MAGIC'S A HOOT

OWL STAR WITCH MYSTERIES BOOK 3

LEANNE LEEDS

Magic's a Hoot
ISBN: 978-1-950505-53-1
Published by Badchen Publishing
14125 W State Highway 29
Suite B-203 119
Liberty Hill, TX 78642 USA

CONTENTS

MAGIC'S A HOOT

CHAPTER ONE

I crawled through the bushes at the edge of Forkbridge Park. My partner, Detective Emma Sullivan, stood at the edge of the playground, watching me look for a necklace that had been reported stolen. How I, the consultant psychic, wound up being the one crawling around in the dirt instead of, you know, the actual detective?

No idea.

It may have been reported stolen, but a quick psychometric chat with the pouch it was kept in told me theft was unlikely. It also told me Carla Laden's six-year-old took it out of the bag and wore it to the playground because she liked the pendant's pretty eyes. Mrs. Laden either left that out of the police report or didn't know.

"Astra, do you see anything?" she asked.

"No," I said, pulling a branch aside so I could get a better look.

Emma sighed heavily and walked back to sit down on a park bench. "I don't know, Astra; this doesn't look how you described it at all. You said the leaves were yellow. Those leaves are green. And you didn't say anything about a see-saw. Are you sure we're in the right park? Are you sure it's even in a park at all?"

I felt my face flush and my hands clench into fists. Ever since Emma's brother—the vampire— had moved to Forkbridge from Las Vegas, there'd been tension between the two of us. Sometimes, intense tension. I'd tried to be patient, to let Emma work out how she felt about her brother's suspicion. Still, my patience was starting to be a tedious thing. Each day that passed, she seemed to treat me just a little bit worse, be just a little more distant. She did not explain it.

But I knew why.

She just didn't know I knew.

First, she never bothered to tell me. Second, Emma didn't know I overheard Rex lambasting her about being friends with witches, because I didn't tell her I heard their fight. She sure didn't think I listened to her valiant defense of my family and me.

A valiant defense she may have made to him, mind you, but which seemed to have put her in a perpetual sour mood with me. A sour mood I was rapidly growing just about sick of.

"I'm doing my best, Emma," I said as I pushed aside a pile of leaves with my foot. "I'm positive this is where it was dropped. Well, in this area, in any case."

"If it was, I guess it's not here now," she said loudly, then glanced around. "Maybe it wasn't stolen at first, but now it is stolen. Someone could have found it and just not turned it in. Technically, it wouldn't really be stolen, but citizens are supposed to turn lost items of value in to the police." She clapped her hands once. "So, I'm comfortable calling this potentially stolen."

Barely, just barely, I saw the tiniest bright flash near the root of the bush. I reached down and brushed the top layer of dead leaves aside, revealing the shiny golden locket. A golden face with red bejeweled eyes stared back at me.

At first, I didn't touch it. This is a town chock full of paranormals, after all.

"You're super creepy," I told the necklace. It

stared back at me with its blank ruby eyes. "Nothing to say, huh?"

I reached out and picked it up—with my gloved hand.

I was brave, not stupid.

Glancing over my shoulder at Emma, I called out, "I've got it," I said. "It's just where I said it would be, oh ye of little faith and annoyingly loud complaints. Okay, necklace obtained. Can we get lunch now?"

I saw the angle of her jaw and her tilting head, and I felt like I was about to not get what I wanted for lunch.

Just a feeling.

Finally, Emma asked, "What do you want?" It sounded like an accusation. Her dark hair, pulled back tightly into a bun, made her expression seem severe. I think she wears it for that reason.

I wanted hamburgers. I told her so.

"Why?" asks Emma.

Why? Really?

She was using her detective's voice, the one she uses with suspects when she wants them to feel guilty for lying to her or for something else they did wrong. Everything, lately, made her question me. Like I'm a perp instead of her friend.

"I dunno. I just do."

Emma looked at me like she's not buying it. I had no idea what there is to buy—or not buy—other than lunch. "What are you going to do after the hamburgers?"

Seriously? I shrugged. "Whatever we need to do, Emma. You're the cop. You tell me."

"I have a better idea for lunch," Emma said. "Let's go to the sushi restaurant down the street."

"Sure. Why not?" I'll go to whatever restaurant she chooses, whether or not it's what I want to eat. Anything to make Emma happy. Anything to keep the ice queen from freezing over because her vampire brother keeps trying to shove ideas in her head that I'm anything other than her friend because I'm a witch. "Sushi works for me," I told her cheerfully.

"Okay," Emma said brightly as she stood up. "Give it back to me for now." She held out her hand, waiting for the necklace.

I handed it back, trying to convince myself she wanted it because she's the cop and I'm just the consultant psychic—and not because her blood-sucking brother had convinced her not to trust me.

THE RESTAURANT WAS CROWDED, but I found an empty booth in the back. I slid in and looked up to see Emma had stopped to chat with an older couple enjoying several plates of raw fish. After a few moments, they shook hands, and she made her way back. Sliding into the seat across from me, she rested her elbows on the table. "This place is great. I used to go to school with the owner."

She looked around. "I like the wood paneling and the old pictures."

I nodded. "It's pretty cool."

It was a long, narrow building with a clean, well-lit interior. The sushi chef had his back to us, but I could see he was rolling sushi with one hand and cutting it with the other.

She smiled. "Look over there. I love the little figurines of the Japanese ladies in kimonos."

"Yeah, I like them too." I looked around the restaurant. "So, how's Rex settling into a place with so much sun? Forkbridge, Florida must be way different from Las Vegas, Nevada. I know they have sun there, too, but it's not exactly known as a daytime city."

"He loves the beach," she said, laughing. "I know, who would have believed that, right? Of course, he only goes at night, but still. He says he loves zipping out there and listening to the sounds of the ocean."

Good.

Maybe he'll drown in the riptide.

Can vampires drown?

I waited, hoping she would finally mention the conversation between them when they were at Arden House for dinner, but she didn't. Emma just looked at the sushi menu and wrote down the rolls she wanted on the pad. As if that was all there was to say about Rex.

But I was done being patient. "What about you? How're you doing with him here?"

Before Emma could answer, the waiter showed up. She ordered a California roll and salmon sashimi for her meal. I ordered yellowtail sashimi and two pieces of eel sushi. The young man asked if we wanted any sake, but we both shook our heads. He scurried away after leaving us with two glasses of ice water.

I assumed Emma would answer me after the waiter left, but she didn't.

"How's your mom doing?" Emma asked me as if trying to change the subject.

"Okay, I think I've had about enough of this," I

told her shortly, throwing down a straw wrapper. She stared at me, her eyes wide. Like she had no idea what I was talking about. Like my annoyance was somehow a surprise. "I've been dancing around this ever since you and Rex had your big blowout, and I've waited for you to talk to me about it, but I feel like that's never going to happen."

"Blowout? What blowout?" Emma swallowed nervously. "What are you talking about?"

"Don't treat me like an idiot," I snapped. "Rex jumped all over you the night my mother had the big witch and pixie and vampire and cop kumbaya gathering at Arden House. Archie"—my owl, a "gift" from the goddess Athena—"told me to go listen to the two of you. I heard Rex go off about witches, heard him tell you that you shouldn't trust me. And frankly, ever since then? You've acted pretty much like you can't trust me."

I stared at her as she examined the table. Finally, Emma looked up, and unlike every other time recently, she didn't look away when our eyes met. She even gave me a small smile that said we were still friends somehow despite everything going on between us. "Astra, that's not—"

"If you are about to tell me that you do, in fact,

trust me, I'm going to rip this glove off my hand and read your throat," I warned her, furious. "You've been a complete jerk to me going on a month now."

"I have not! I am trying to—"

"Make me feel like your inferior? Keep me at arm's length? Push me away? Make me quit? What?"

Emma looked at me for a long time before she spoke. "Fine. I don't know how to fix this, anyway. But my brother is using the vampire blood bond to watch me when we're together. We, you and I, I mean. He's watching everything," she said at last. "So, I've been acting like I don't trust you, like we're not friends, hoping that he sees I don't trust you and will leave you alone. Even though I do trust you, and we are friends." She half-smiled. "If that makes any sense."

"No. It doesn't." I sighed. "But then again, it kind of does. He can keep tabs on you even when he's asleep during the day? Seriously?" She nodded. "I know he loves you and all but jeez, Emma. That's a level of in-your-business that's got to be hard to take."

"I don't trust people," Emma said. "I never have. I find it hard to believe anything that they say. He knows that, and, to be honest, he's kind of using that to try and convince me not to trust you. Not because of who you are, but because of what you are. Honestly, Astra, dealing with it is just exhausting. I think I have PTSD from seeing the moon rise at this point. And I hate it, I do. But..." Emma held up her hands.

"But he's your brother."

"He's my brother." She sighed. "I do trust you, Astra. I really do. I'm just doing the best I can here."

I tilted my head and stared at my friend. "Maybe I shouldn't even ask this. But why?"

"Why am I doing my best?" she asked, confused. "Or why do I trust you?"

"You're doing your best because you're Emma Sullivan, and you can't do things any other way," I told her with a half-smile. "Trusting me. Why do you trust me? I'm just curious." Rex, no doubt, had filled her head with all sorts of accusations against me, all kinds of things I'd done when I was a fugitive tracker for the Witches' Council.

"I don't know. Instinct? I just do."

"Then maybe you should tell your brother to go suck on a tourist and butt out." I didn't say it harshly or spitefully; I simply stated it as a fact, but Emma winced as if the words had been vicious. "Aw, look, I'm sorry. I shouldn't have said that. I don't want to be the other side of a tug of war over your feelings. And I do get it. Rex is your brother. I have no doubt that he means well, but I'm upset he's putting you in this position. I wish he'd just come at me directly."

Emma was silent for a moment, thinking about what I'd said, then she shook her head. "No, Astra."

I blinked innocently. "No, what?"

"You're going to confront him. I can tell."

"No," I said. "I'm going to talk to him, but I'm not going to confront him."

"I don't know, Astra." She tucked a strand of hair behind her ear, but the motion was jerky. Like she was nervous.

Seeing Emma Sullivan nervous was so jarring it made me want to punch the vampire brother right in the face. Emma had nerves of steel. Rex was twisting her apart the way only family could.

I shrugged. "Look, I just want to talk to him. I feel like he needs to know what's happening. Well, he knows what's happening, but I don't think he realizes the toll it's taking on you. How can he? The man naps all day. It's not like I'm going to do anything to him." Even though I could. Oh, I really could.

Emma looked at me suspiciously, as if she'd heard my murderous thought.

"I'm not! I just want him to know. And I want to give him the chance to say what he has to say to me. Directly." I leaned forward and stared deep into Emma's eyes. "You know. Like a man."

She stared at me and then laughed in spite of herself. "You totally did that on purpose," Emma accused, still chuckling. "You know he's probably listening to this whole conversation, and you did that on purpose just to poke at him."

"Darn skippy, I did," I muttered under my breath. Just then, the waiter came with plates.

I tried not to think about the fact that the disposable wooden chopsticks would double nicely as stakes for a vampire.

I PACED BACK and forth as the sky went from orange to purple. Despite Emma's warning, I waited for Rex at the entrance to his underground compound. Well, it was barely underground. And truth be told, it was scarcely a compound. He just threw dirt on a storm shelter and called it a day.

But, you know, to each vampire his own, I guess.

I wasn't scared. I knew that I had to confront him.

But I brought Althea's anti-vampire repellent. Just in case.

I wasn't stupid.

In the distance, deep within the property he bought, I saw a flash of red. It was the color of blood, and for a moment, I tensed. Despite my anger at Rex, I didn't relish getting into a physical fight with Emma's brother, even if I was sure I could win. Emma was going through enough without me adding "murdered your already dead brother" to the list of family issues.

I also didn't know whether Rex was one of those blood bank vampires, or if he just randomly grabbed some annoying tourist off the street for nourishment. If that red flash was a tourist getting slurped up, I'd have to get involved, and taking a meal from a vampire wouldn't be a good start to this conversation. As the red grew closer, I relaxed. It was Rex's jacket.

Blood red.

Of course it was.

"Hey, Astra," he said with a bit of a smile. "What's up?"

"You know what's up."

"Do I?" he asked evenly.

The vampire didn't seem bothered in the least I was there. In fact, he seemed utterly at ease.

He did, though, stop his approach several feet from me to sweep his eyes up and down my form. Looking for weapons, Dracula? Trying to judge the defensive capabilities of my magical "Black Widow" cosplay outfit, as Emma called it? Figuring out which part of my exposed skin you'll head toward first if something goes down?

He raised an eyebrow and stretched casually. "You came to see me, Astra. Not the other way around. If you have something to say, why don't you say it so we can both get on with our evening."

I bit back a snarky response. His bored, dismissive tone rankled me.

"I wanted to talk to you about Emma." You know exactly why I'm here, you overbearing, misogynistic, blood-drinking buffoon. Do you really want to stand here in the dark and play games?

He couldn't read my mind thanks to my military-issued outfit, but part of me wished he could.

"What's wrong with Emma?" Rex asked as he leaned against a tree, unconcerned.

I felt a moment of regret for not bringing the chopsticks.

"She is your sister. You know what's wrong with her." I stepped forward. "Quit playing coy. The innocent act is not cute, and I don't have the patience to play games."

"Fine," he said. Something in his face subtly changed, and there was the sudden gleam of resentment in his eyes. "You have a question? Ask me anything."

Ask him?

Was he not grown up enough to just tell me how he felt?

"Fine. Why do you hate women?" I'd groped for something to knock him off his disinterest, and I may have found it because the vampire looked surprised. But I didn't think I was wrong, either—his not trusting witches was understandable. He was a vampire, and witches and vampires aren't exactly buddies. But the way he treated his sister, the lack of respect for her independence? The boundary-pushing? The refusal to listen to her, to talk through things? The demand she do what he said?

Vampire or not, the dude was a misogynist.

And it was abusive.

He eyed me for a moment and then laughed.

"That's your big question?" he asked. His tone was light and teasing. "Come on, Astra. I mean, really? I thought you'd have something better after everything I heard today."

I didn't crack a smile. "You're toying with me instead of having a conversation with me. There's nothing better to ask. I want to know why you hate women." My fists were clenched. I was appalled at Emma's brother's attitude—and I secretly hoped that my anti-vampire repellent was still hanging where I thought it was.

"I don't hate women," he said, lightly skimming his hand over his shirt, smoothing out imaginary lint.

"Of course you do," I said. "You treat your sister like a child, like she doesn't know how to make her own decisions. You talk about me to her, but you never bother to come to me. It never occurred to you to talk out your issues with me. You think you know better than both of us, know more about us than we know about ourselves." His eyes narrowed, and his smile faltered. "Okay, maybe you don't hate women, but you sure don't respect them at all."

"This isn't about the two of you being women!" he protested hotly.

"Your sister is faking the tone of our friendship to me because she's afraid you'll see how she honestly feels, thinks, and acts around me." Rex pulled himself off the tree and tensed. I felt the instinctive urge to step back. "How can you possibly be okay with that? Knowing that you being inside her head is not a comfort, but something she feels she needs to hide from? That she's afraid of? How are you any different from an abusive, controlling boyfriend that punishes a grown woman like a child for the wrong behavior?"

As those words poured from my mouth, I realized I wasn't thinking of them as I said them. They came from my gut. A sensible part of me said that I should keep my mouth shut and back off him a little bit, but the dominant voice in my head told me to push Rex so he'd see what he was doing to Emma.

"How can you say that? How can you even think that way?" he told me hotly. "I would never abuse Emma. Never!"

"I never said that you did it deliberately," I replied coldly, "but you sure aren't offering her the trust or respect she deserves from you. And your constant badgering and spying are making her life miserable."

"How can you be so naive, acting like I have no reason to be concerned?" he asked. "You're a witch, aren't you? Use some of that magic to figure this out for yourself. Why do you think I'm so afraid for her around you and your family?" Rex raised an eyebrow and tilted his head. He looked so much like Emma when he did that. I wanted to like him.

Right now, though, I just didn't.

I pulled my head back and clenched my teeth. "Why are you giving me a guilt trip like who and what I am, who my family is, is somehow my fault, something I have to apologize for? You're the one who's wrong here. Full stop. I've done nothing but help Emma in her career, work with her on cold cases, and be a friend to her. I've given her space to work out whatever the heck it is you're putting her through, because she's a grown up, and I trust her. And, by the way, I never told her, not once, to avoid her murderous, blood-sucking, mobbed-up criminal brother because he might be bad for her. Not once!"

That set him back on his heels, and the vampire looked at me with that expressionless thousand-yard stare that told me nothing about what he was thinking. After a minute, maybe two, he finally spoke. "You obviously don't know what you are talking about."

"Maybe you're right. Maybe I don't." I didn't try to mask the sadness and frustration in my voice. "But Emma is my best friend. I'd never let anything happen to her if I could prevent it. But that's the issue, Rex—she's a grown woman, ex-military, and she carries a gun. If we were in a situation where I could protect her, I would. The likelihood that she'd need that protection, though?" I held up my hands. "Pretty damn low."

"You and I are both much more powerful than she is—"

"There! Right there! See?" The anger was coursing through my blood now—itchy, bitter, and painful. I pointed. "You don't respect her! Emma is not a wilting flower, Rex!"

I felt a spark of magic run up my arm and straight into my fingertips.

Huh.

Rex stared at my hand in horror. "What the hell was that?"

"Um. Energy," I told him. I ran my hand through my hair. "That's why so many witches have crazy hair, isn't it?" I laughed uncomfortably. "Static, maybe."

He didn't answer.

And the truth was I had no idea—no idea at all —what that was.

But I would not admit that to him.

The vampire shifted from one foot to the other. "Look. I know she's not a wilting flower. I'm just saying she needs to understand the situation."

I raised an eyebrow. "I didn't realize that she wasn't aware of it already. I'm a witch. My family? They're witches. What else is there?"

He glared at me.

And suddenly, I realized this might never work.

Well, not with this approach.

"I'm sorry," I said suddenly.

That shocked him. "For what?"

"For not realizing I can't fix this by badgering you the way you badger her. We need to stop badgering each other and change the way we're dealing with all this."

"What does that mean?"

I took a breath, watching his face harden, and answered honestly. "Unless you give me—and my family—a chance, you're never going to trust me around Emma. You're never going to trust her around us. But that's something only you can choose to do. We're not the Las Vegas witches that screwed you over, Rex," I told him (taking a shot in the dark). "Until you can try to see that, though? You're going to keep putting Emma in the middle of this."

He glared at me again.

"And that," I added, "is the only paranormal thing truly hurting her right now."

CHAPTER TWO

"*N*o one's going to ask how it went?" I asked my family. My sisters—Ami, Althea, and Ayla—piled together like puppies on the couch watching some K-pop band on the big screen television. Mom and Aunt Gwennie sat at the dining table behind them, grinding something in mortars with pestles.

"We know how it went, dear," Aunt Gwennie said distractedly, her nose in a book laying flat on the table. "Your owl beat you home by about twenty minutes, and it doesn't take very much time to say 'bad.'" She waved toward the window. "He wanted us to let you know he was going out for the night. I am glad you and the vampire didn't engage in a physical confrontation. Emma would have been quite put out about that."

I grabbed a Ziploc bag full of garlic bread from the dinner I missed and slid into a chair at the table. "It was fine. I had Althea's vampire repellent. I wouldn't have hurt him." I took a bite of garlic bread and chewed. The bread was delicious, even cold. "Much," I added with my mouth full.

"I did warn you, Astra. I know all of you paranormals lived together in Imperatorial City as if those old grievances of the past were long gone, but outside of Impy?" Mom looked up and frowned. "Things are still tense, much to my dismay. And provoking a vampire is not the wisest course of action. They can be very impulsive."

I shook my head. "I can handle Rex Sullivan."

Aunt Gwennie put her hand on my arm. "You don't know that, Astra. I know you're strong, but you don't know what you're up against. How many vampires did you actually go after when you were in the Ministry?"

More than my aunt could possibly conceive of. The Witches' Council seemed to have a special place in their dungeon for vampires that wouldn't bend the knee—and that was pretty much all of them. "I don't want to fight the guy, Auntie. I just want to get him to stop having whatever knee-jerk reaction the dude is having about us, just because we're witches."

"Well, have you asked him why he feels the way he does, dear?" she asked.

I shrugged. "I didn't think it was any of my business. His feelings are his feelings, and he can have them from now until the pixie alligators come home. All I care about is how he's making Emma miserable and, by extension, how he's making me miserable."

Aunt Gwennie gave a rap on the tabletop with her knuckles. "No, it's not your business. But you might have a better chance of convincing him to change his mind if you could find out why he feels the way he does. I wouldn't even suggest you ask him; it's too personal, considering the hostility between you. You'd have to gain his confidence to find out what it is."

I burst out laughing. I mean, really laughed. "Gain his confidence? I told him the only way to get over himself was to get to know us. To see we weren't some mortal threat to his sister."

"And what did he say?" my mother asked me, looking up.

"Nothing. Not a thing. He just walked away.

But it didn't look like it was something he was considering. Then again, they're not exactly demonstrative."

I watched my family as they continued comparing notes and discussing strategies regarding Rex in a lighthearted way. There was nothing they could tell me, of course. They were saying things like "give it time" and "see how everything works out" and "we only live once, but vampires twice and the second time live long enough to make everything complicated." It was all very cliché and practical.

And useless.

"Oh, by the way, while I was talking to him? My fingers sparked."

That turned their eyes my way in a hurry. All ten eyes, five pairs. All on me.

"What do you mean 'sparked?'" my mother asked.

"I don't know where they were coming from, but they were like little white fireworks coming off my fingers. I don't know how to describe it better than that. My fingers just sparked. Like a tiny fireworks display." I popped another piece of garlic bread in my mouth. "What, Archie didn't mention that? He must have seen it."

"No, dear," Aunt Gwennie said.

"He didn't mention it at all? Are you sure?"

"Yes, dear, I'm sure."

I wondered if I should be concerned about that.

"WHY IS that card glowing like that?" Gloria Fisher asked, her voice echoing with alarm. "Is it supposed to do that?"

I'd gotten a text that morning from Emma telling me she had to do some training with something or another for her certification. She encouraged me to stay home from my job as a police consultant that day. I tried not to be suspicious that Rex went straight over to see her the night before, and my discussion with him had made things worse.

I sent her a smiley face and a comment that the day off would be great. Emma didn't respond.

But maybe the goddess does work in mysterious ways. It was thanks to the impromptu day off I happened to be sitting at the counter in Athena's Garden, my family's new age/craft/herb store when Ami's tarot reading produced the glowing Star card.

The glowing Star card, for those that have

forgotten, is either a message from the goddess Athena that someone's about to die and she wants me to keep it from happening or a complicated spell my mother cooked up to give me something to do now that I'd been forcibly retired from my lifetime military position.

"Why is it sticking to my husband's card like that?" Gloria asked my sister. "Is there glue on it?" Suddenly angry, she snapped, "I'm not paying extra for your trickery, you know! You said the reading was twenty dollars, and I don't care how many cards light up. I'm not paying a penny more than that!"

I stood up and made my way over to the corner reading area to help Ami deal with Gloria's impending meltdown.

As I rounded the corner, though, Ami's expression was clear and steady, as if she hadn't heard the woman's cranky attack. "How long have you been married?" she asked Gloria in a voice so kind it made me blink.

"Twenty-three years," Gloria responded, hanging back now but still pouting unhappily. "And he's always drinking quite heavily, and you're right to be worried about him. It's why I came in here, even though I don't believe in any of this. One of my girlfriends said you might be able to help, but…" Gloria burst into tears. "This is just silly. I don't know why I came here."

This woman could change emotional gears as rapidly as an Italian sports car.

"Astra, look," Ami said, pointing to the cards on the table. "The Star card came up on top of the card for her husband, and every time I try to move it? Watch." My sister pulled the glowing card off the reading and placed it to the side of the table on its own. Two seconds later, it slid like a planchette on a Ouija board right back onto the Knight of Pentacles. "That's happened three times now. I don't think it's her." Ami looked up at me. "I think it's him."

"What's him? What are the two of you talking about?" Gloria asked, her voice panicky. As she spoke, the card moved again, fully covering the Knight. "Why is that happening? Are you trying to get more money out of me? I was warned about the curse con, you know, so don't you even try and tell me William's cursed."

Okay. I won't tell you.

But Ami was correct—it looked like the Star card was trying to get across a danger to Gloria's husband and not her.

"See?" Ami said, handing the Star card to me. "It has to be him."

I took the card and looked at it. "Maybe."

"No!" Gloria said, shoving the cards on the table into a jumble back toward Ami. "I don't like this! No, it doesn't feel right. Take these back. I don't want the extra mystical reading you two are concocting. Just a regular one." Gloria nodded as if that settled it. "Thank you."

The cards sprang back into their former positions in the blink of an eye.

Gloria Fisher stared at the table, horrified.

"Relax, Gloria," I said, tucking the card under the Knight of Pentacles. "What does your husband do for a living? Where does he work?"

Her face took on a look of suspicion as she placed her hands flat on the table. "Aren't you supposed to be answering my questions? This must be a con. You're trying to trick me." She looked at each of us. "I've changed my mind. I don't want your readings. No, I changed my mind! I just want to go now. This wasn't even worth twenty dollars."

She was halfway to the door before Ami and I jumped into action.

"Gloria, wait! Let me explain!" Ami said, reaching out to her. But as soon as the words left her lips, we heard the door open and slam shut. Gloria was gone.

Ami turned to me. "Okay, so I'm starting to think we should have a plan for how to handle star people that are less than believers. This is the third time the Star card has come up. Two out of three times, the person it hit on basically ran screaming from the shop." My sister crossed her arms. "That's not a very good track record, Astra."

Before I could answer, Archie flew in through the back window. "We got a card?"

I raised my eyebrow. "How did you know?"

"I am the goddess's own owl, a divine being that can feel a disturbance in the Force, you know!" the owl told me, quoting Star Wars. "How could you even ask me that? I'm insulted! Insulted, I tell you!" Lightning struck outside as if on cue, its flash of energy illuminating the room in pure white for an instant.

Ami gasped. Archie looked pleased.

I stared at the owl.

Archie's dark eyes watched me intently.

I silently raised my eyebrow again.

Finally, he shrugged his wings. "Fine. The woman that ran out of here looked completely freaked out about something, and I didn't think it was the price of the blue calcite."

"It's a shame Emma isn't available to help look up information on William Fisher," Aunt Gwennie said. My entire family gathered around the table. You would think the Star card was a bat signal, and we were the Justice League. Wait. Batman was in the Justice League, right? Or am I thinking of the Avengers? Did they have a bat signal?

Anyway, my entire family mobilized into action.

"But why do I have to watch the shop?" Ayla, thirteen, complained as soon as my mother directed her to take over for Ami and me. "I have ghost spies all over Forkbridge, you know! I could get information about Will Fisher—his friends call him Will, by the way—faster than you could get it off the internet!"

Mom looked at her dubiously. "Fine," my mother said with a tired sigh. "I'll leave you to it. The priority is to keep an eye on Will while your sister's getting her information. Tell the ghosts that. How long will that take you?"

The excitement lit up her face, and she shimmered like a new coin as she grinned. "Like, two seconds! No time at all!"

"Fantastic. After that, go watch the store. And Ayla, don't think I didn't catch you admitting you talk to ghosts behind my back," my mother warned her with a stern look. "You and I are going to have a talk later."

Her face fell. "Yeah, yeah," Ayla said with an eye roll. I was impressed with Ayla's tacit acceptance of my mother's ability to give an inch while keeping that mile firmly in her pocket. Then with a conspiratorial eye roll in my direction, she whispered, "You get all the fun because you're the oldest."

"No, I get all the fun because I see traps like that coming and avoid them," I whispered back. "You walked into that one."

"Yeah, yeah, I know," Ayla said with a sigh. Then she raced out of the room to talk to her ghost friends.

"Do you think I should call Detective Sullivan?" Ami asked as she leaned on the back counter. "Maybe she's avoiding you because of the Rex thing, and my contact will be less pressure on her."

While the others were digging up information on Will, Ami and I were trying to figure out how to handle an investigation into William Fisher's potential death. You know, without police help, and without Gloria Fisher's trust that we were poking around her life for a perfectly good reason.

"I've already sent Emma three texts," I told Ami, holding up my phone. "I'm guessing she's either ignoring me or seriously in the middle of training. I can catch her after work." When Rex would, no doubt, have his evening chat. The one where he would go on ad infinitum about the dangers of being friends with witches. "You know, Rex was instrumental on the last case with his super-spy hearing. I wish he wasn't such a jerk about all this. I could think of a hundred ways he would be really useful."

I was so angry at Rex, the one positive statement I made about him felt like ashes in my mouth.

"Speaking of the vampire, did you see the paper this morning?" Althea, sixteen, asked me, looking up from the laptop where she was uncovering all the public dirt on Will Fisher. "Rex just bought that abandoned warehouse. You know, the one right past Parrot Wildwoods on Circle Boot Lane? That big gray one that used to be the furniture store."

"Rex was in the newspaper?" I asked, surprised. Emma told me her parents (who still lived in the Forkbridge area) believed Rex was dead. In fact, it was one of the major issues between the two siblings. Well, an issue that appeared to have nothing to do with witches, in any case. Emma thought Rex should tell her parents he was a vampire. Rex thought Emma was off her rocker. "Did they say he was...well, him?"

"A vampire?" Althea asked, surprised. "No."

"Not a vampire. That he was from Forkbridge."

Althea held up her hand and tilted it from side to side. "His name, but not that he was from Forkbridge originally."

Huh. Interesting. "Did the article say why he bought it?"

"He's opening up a nightclub. And get this— he's naming it 'Sanguine.'" Althea made a face. "I mean, I get it. Not much else a vampire can do since they only come out at night, right? But still. A nightclub in Forkbridge? I just wouldn't think the town would be all that jazzed about it. This isn't Orlando. How're they going to make money?"

"Yeah, crazy," I murmured and looked out at the backyard.

Where did Rex get the money to buy—and renovate—a warehouse into a nightclub?

"You've got that look on your face," Ami said quietly. "What are you thinking?"

"I don't know," I said as I watched the breeze blow through the hibiscus in the garden. I looked back at Ami. "I just wonder where he got all the money for it. That place is huge. That's not cheap."

"No," Althea said quietly. "No, I would imagine it isn't."

"Looks like he's staying in town permanently."

Ami nodded. "Looks like."

Great.

CHAPTER THREE

I was the only customer in the small waiting room of the Barber Insurance Agency, a storefront in what would likely be considered the "unsavory" part of town.

Well, if Forkbridge had an unsavory part of town.

Which it didn't. The stores were less than sparkling and new, the homes wrapped with sun-faded colors and peeling paint. The streets contained potholes that no one even complained about anymore.

But it was still mostly adorable.

The walls of the insurance office, at least, were a bright white, as if trying to give it that

Florida beachy vibe. It was the only thing about the place that didn't seem dingy.

Yellowed posters hung forlornly on some walls: one had a picture of a house being attacked by lightning, a tornado, and a fire simultaneously. The one next to it was just a message reminding you that you can never, ever be too protected. The last? A silhouette of a family and another reminder: insurance agents are there to protect your family when you're not able to. They were not framed, just stuck into the shiplap with push pins.

Cheerful.

Two voices, muffled, talked in the back office. I listened.

One was a woman's. The other was a man's. They were both slightly slurred and somewhat indistinct—as if the five o'clock bourbons started well before lunch.

You know, a real classy place.

"Hello?" I called loudly, hoping to get someone's attention.

A few moments later, a man emerged from the back. He was a tall man with thinning black hair. He walked up to me and leaned down, so his face was just inches from mine. His eyes appeared bloodshot, and his rolled up sleeves showed off a collection of band-aids all over his arms. "I'm sorry," he said. "We're closed." The man's breath hit my face like a cloud of smoke from a cigarette.

I coughed.

He frowned.

"I'm waiting for William Fisher," I said. "I was hoping to get some insurance. Are you Mr. Fisher?"

The man shook his head and stepped back. "No," he said, "Will Fisher's on vacation."

Vacation? I frowned. Gloria said nothing about Will being on vacation. That could complicate things. Can't precisely search the internet for where someone's gone on vacation.

Well. Not legally.

"Oh," I said. "I see. I'll just need to come back, then." I stood up, turned, and reached for the door.

"But," the man said, "I can help you." The man then pulled a cap from behind him and placed it on his head, smoothing down his thinning hair and the sides of his face. The hat said Barber Insurance Agency. He smiled, looking pleased with himself.

"You can?" I asked. "I mean, I guess you could. I'm not sure how, exactly. A friend recommended William specifically."

The man stepped forward. "My name is Charles," he said, extending his hand. "Charles Fisher."

Fisher, huh? "Are you Will's brother?"

My question rattled him. It shouldn't have. It was a logical question. "N-n-n-n-no. Me? No," Charles stammered. He pulled back his hand, glancing nervously about. "No," he said again, his voice stronger. "No, no, I...my...I'm not his brother. Why would you think that?"

Because you have the same last name?

"Sorry about that," I told him, outwardly accepting his answer. I could tell you that my honed super-senses picked up on Charles's lie, or my psychic institution was so strong the lie seeped through my gloves and straight into my brain. The simple fact is the guy was a nervous wreck. A three-year-old would have known this guy was Will's brother and that he was hiding something.

"That's fine." Charles shrugged and took a swig from a bottle he pulled from his pocket.

This place started classy and was getting more refined by the minute. "So you're actually an insurance agent, too, then?" I asked. He nodded. "I've been talking to Gloria."

The drunken agent looked at me. "Gloria's Will's wife."

"You don't say!" I feigned surprise.

Charles shook his head. "No, I did say," he told me, giving me a look like I was a little dense. "Anyway, yeah, I work here." He stepped back to offer me a rickety chair in front of what looked like the receptionist's desk.

"Doing what?" I asked, taking my seat. "Just doing insurance?"

"Yes, ma'am," Charles said. "So what did you—"

"So William is your boss?" I asked.

Charles nodded. "Yes, ma'am. What kind of—"

"That must be nice. Do you live in town?" I asked.

Charles shook his head. "I live here in Florida with my mother," he said. "But over by Disney World."

"So you drive up here every day?" I asked. "That's a long drive to work at such a small agency. Is it just you and Will here by yourselves?"

Charles nodded even as someone moved around in the back office.

Everything about this agency just screamed

sketchy—the location. The mirrored windows preventing anyone from looking in—which made sense if your space was filled with booze-addled agents in a sparsely decorated office. The lie Charles told about being Will's brother—I mean, I'd confirm it later, but I'd bet my owl on the fact that they were brothers. I'd also bet my owl Charles was hiding it.

Why lie to some random stranger off the street?

Just then, my phone buzzed. I glanced down at the text from Ami. *Emma is here at the house. You need to come back here.* I sent back a question mark. *Just get here as soon as you can.* Ami texted me nothing more, and the phone fell silent.

"I have to go," I told Charles and held up my phone. "Work emergency." I had no idea how true that flippant statement would be.

As I got up, I reached out and slipped an ashtray from the receptionist's desk into my pocket.

"Sure thing," Charles said, looking relieved and not noticing the theft. "Take care."

I nodded, exited the office, and ran back to my Jeep. As I jumped in, gunned the engine, and left the parking lot, I paused before I turned. Huh. What kind of insurance agent looks relieved he didn't sell an insurance policy?

I WALKED into the house and found Emma sitting at the kitchen table. Aunt Gwennie stood at the counter behind her with a bouquet of flowers, carefully removing petals for one of her tinctures. Ami stood in the kitchen, her face tense.

Well, this didn't look good. I wondered, grumpily, what Rex did now.

"So, how was your day?" I asked, sitting next to the detective, a feigned cheerfulness wrapping my question in a cotton candy optimism I didn't quite feel. "Training go okay?"

She smiled, but it seemed strained.

I smiled back wider.

Her smile faltered.

I raised my eyebrow. I'd never seen her look so serious.

"So, I have to talk to you about something. I know how this is going to sound, but just hear me out. Okay? Just listen to everything all the way through before reacting." Emma shook her head sadly and stared at the floor for a moment. Finally, she said, "I've been in a meeting this whole morning with the police captain." She met my eyes. "Rex made a complaint."

I shrugged. I gave precisely two figs about Rex

Sullivan and his complaints. "From what I can tell, your brother has a list of complaints as long as my arm. But okay, I'll bite. A complaint about what? And to who?"

"You. He said you've been harassing him," Emma continued. "He submitted a formal complaint last night, in writing, to the department. It went straight to the captain."

I stared at her. I still didn't understand what she was telling me. "He said I've been what now?"

She tensed as if to prepare for a struggle and said, "He said you keep asking him to go out with you, and he feels harassed by your repeated requests." Her tone made it clear she didn't believe it, but it also clarified that whether Emma believed it or not? That wasn't the central issue now.

For a moment, my mind felt numb, as if everything inside me had been frozen. Then a warmth overtook me. A heat that turned into a red-hot fury. My fingers sparked.

That no-good snake.

Even though I knew it was a long shot, I thought Rex might want to be friends eventually. I thought he might want to get to know me, know my family. We'd worked together during the pixie fiasco. I thought we'd got along. I thought he might want to stop being a completely intolerant, knee-jerk, hyper-reactive bigot at some point.

Apparently, I thought wrong.

This is what I got for approaching him directly?

Embarrassed at my job with a complaint that's a total lie?

I shot up out of the chair so fast it scraped across the floor. Then I paced. "Your brother is off the rails, Emma."

She sighed. "I know." Emma stared into my eyes so I could see how sorry she was.

Her sadness only made me angrier.

I laughed sarcastically. "Me? Go out with him? He's lucky I don't stake him, that blood-sucking—"

"Astra," Aunt Gwennie said sharply. "Be nice."

I whirled on my aunt. "Are you kidding me? Why the heck should I be nice? He's lying about me, Aunt Gwen. And he's trying to get me fired! This is beyond the pale. I didn't ask him to go out with me. I asked him to stop making his sister absolutely miserable." I narrowed my eyes. "Did he buy a nightclub just so he'd have standing in the town to make a complaint about me and have it jumped on? I wouldn't put it past that piece of—"

"Astra." Aunt Gwennie's voice was like steel.

"Listen. The captain is willing to let it go if you apologize to Rex," Emma said. "We can fix this."

I turned and stared at Emma. "I'm sorry. What did you say? Can you repeat that? Because I'm sure, I didn't hear you correctly. Apologize for what?"

Emma looked uncomfortable, but her voice was steady. "You can apologize to Rex, and we can all put this behind us. I doubt he'll pull the same scheme twice, so...just apologize, Astra. Pretend you're apologizing for going over there last night." She looked down. "If you don't, you might actually get fired. I tried to explain it, I really did, but there's a huge amount of information I can't tell the captain, and you know that." She paused, waiting for a response. "In the end, you're not a cop; you don't have a union. You just don't have the same protections I do." Another pause. "And sexual harassment is a big deal now."

Sure.

Thanks to Emma and me, sexual harassment had been prioritized at the station.

Now they take it seriously.

Way to go, Forkbridge Police.

I stared at Emma, shocked that was the best ending to the situation she could come up with. One in which I effectively admit to sexually harassing a vampire? Are you kidding? For a moment, my anger flared at Emma—she was my partner, my backup. How could she expect me to apologize? Emma shook her head sadly, as if she heard the angry thoughts racing through my mind.

My anger fizzled.

Standing up for me would've meant taking my side over Rex's side.

If there was one thing Emma couldn't do, it was that.

At least not yet.

And Rex darn well knew it.

I took a deep breath as my fingers sparked with a sizzle. "I'm not apologizing to him. He's trying to humiliate me with a lie. No one—and I mean no one—has the right to do something like this to me." Emma wouldn't even look at me. She kept her eyes on Aunt Gwennie. "Emma, I know he's your brother, and I know you love him, but I won't apologize to someone that's abusing other people to get what he wants. To force others to bend to his will. I can't do it. It's not in me."

Aunt Gwennie stood in front of me with that firm-lipped, you're-being-stubborn but-I-still-love-you look she got sometimes. "You realize the captain may have no choice but to let you go?"

"I figure that's exactly what's going to happen," I told my aunt. "It doesn't change anything. I won't be manipulated into doing something I know is wrong or apologizing to someone I think is wrong. I was in the military too long doing too many things that keep me up at night now to let Rex Sullivan do something like this to me again." I looked at Emma. "I'm sorry. I've loved working with you, Emma. If this is how it ends, I don't regret anything."

Except not stabbing your brother with a chopstick last night, I thought to myself. I'm regretting that a little bit.

"I'm so sorry, Astra," she whispered.

I didn't know whether to laugh or cry.

In the end, I did neither. I just turned and walked out of the room.

It was a massive victory for Rex and a humiliating loss for me. I felt like a fool for miscalculating the lengths the vampire would go to. I wouldn't make that mistake again.

But if he thought this was over?

Oh, boy, he had another think coming.

I just…didn't know what that was.

Yet.

"I UNDERSTAND, CHIEF," I told Chief Harmon.

"Astra, I wish there was something else I could do," he told me sincerely. "But the sexual harassment rules we came up with dictate terminating any contractor that's even suspected of this." He sniffed. "Maybe we went a little overboard with the rules in this case. I certainly never thought—well, anyway."

The chief sounded genuinely regretful as he told me my services were no longer needed at the Forkbridge Police Department. I'm sure he was— since I showed up, cold cases from years past had been closed like the doors in a stable after a horse race. I solved cases and found stolen objects no one else could, and at a bottom-dollar investigative rate.

And now, all of that was over.

An hour after that phone call, to add insult to injury, a courier arrived with a formal letter from the city. "Ms. Arden," the letter began. "Due to recent events, your contract with the Forkbridge PD is being terminated immediately. You will be responsible for returning all city and private equipment and property in your possession upon termination of your contract. The charges for services rendered under your contract will be paid within thirty days."

I fought the urge to take the paper and shove it down Rex Sullivan's blood-sucking throat.

"So what happens now?" Ami asked me.

"Now?" I folded the letter and stuck it in my back pocket. "Now we find out why someone wants Will Fisher dead, and we stop him from dying. We still have a job to do. It just doesn't pay as well."

"Are you okay with all this?" she asked, her expression concerned.

I laughed.

I laughed so hard I had to hold my sides and lean against the counter for support.

Ami reached out, her face twisted in confusion as if she thought I had finally snapped. I waved her off. "I'm fine. I am, I'm fine. I just…a vampire just got me fired. My best friend has a controlling brother spying on her from the dead. And we have to save the life of some sketchy, drunken insurance salesman I can't even find.

No, Ami. I am so not okay with any of this." I wiped my eyes. "I wish I could follow ties like that witch in Mystic's End could—hey." I blinked. "Wait a minute."

"What?" Ami asked. "Did you come up with something?"

"I did. Ooh, I really did," I laughed evilly. "I've got an idea."

Ami stared at me. "Wow. That was manic. What's up?"

"I'm going to solve the problem," I said, my eyes lighting up. "I'm going to mess with Rex's game so hard. He thinks he's got all the information, all the control? Come on, let's go talk to Althea."

I raced up the stairs, Ami hot on my heels, and made a sharp right turn on the second floor. Sticking my head into Althea's bedroom, I called out, "You busy?" She looked up from her computer and shook her head no. "Can you do me a favor?"

"Sure, what's up?" Althea looked at us.

"Okay, potion master. Find me a way to break the vampire blood bond with a human," I told her in a determined tone.

His open door into Emma's head?

Let's see how he does when I slam it shut.

CHAPTER FOUR

$\mathcal{I}$ sat on the floor in my attic bedroom, the stolen ashtray in my hands. The most important moments in the depressing storefront were locked inside it.

There was one clear benefit to not being employed by the police department anymore.

I could steal things now.

The ashtray was heavy in my palm. The word *Believe* etched on one side in a font similar to one you might find on the sign for a fake English pub in New York. "Okay, buddy, what have you seen?" I whispered to it. "You're glass, so I'm expecting great things from you. You hear me?"

The glass didn't answer.

I took off my glove, placed it beside me, and

grasped the ashtray. Its surface was smooth to the touch. As I closed my eyes, the psychic (or psychometric, if you want to get specific) images flooded into my mind almost immediately.

A desk.

The receptionist's desk? It had to be, there were the posters on the walls.

There was a man sitting at the desk, but I didn't know him. It could be Will Fisher. I thought I could spot a slight resemblance to Charles Fisher—though this guy wasn't as greasy looking. His suit and tie were freshly pressed or ironed.

The man stared at a stack of papers on the desk in front of him. He looked like he was concentrating on something, because he had his tongue stuck out a little and was frowning.

Just as he was about to speak, the image dissolved.

I raced after it, but my mind went black.

Then, a second later, Emma's face.

"Oh, come on!" I complained. "If you've got something to show me, show me!" Emma went from a vague image to a distinct one. Her lips moved, so she must be speaking but I couldn't hear anything.

Her face gave way to the man again, still concentrating.

A second later, Emma again.

"Come on! Stop playing games," I pleaded. I didn't know if I was talking to the goddess, my power, my own subconscious, or the ashtray itself. Whatever I was talking to, none of the above seemed to listen. "Just show me what I need to know. This isn't funny anymore."

As if in a huff, the images withdrew with a finality.

I opened my eyes and glared at the cheap piece of glass with resentment. I got fired, outwitted by a mobbed-up vampire, and I couldn't even focus long enough to hear the words in a vision, much less hold the darn thing in place.

Wait.

I didn't need to hear anything in the vision. The man never spoke. It was Emma who'd been talking, and I know she'd probably never been in the insurance office, so… No, wait. The man was about to talk. I just lost focus before he spoke. I dropped the ashtray on the floor.

What on earth was wrong with me today?

Looking around, I suddenly realized my room

was a mess. Maybe that was the problem. How could anyone work in a place that was this dirty? Probably just breaking my concentration. There were clothes everywhere, and the rugs I'd placed on the hardwood floor had dust and feathers all over them thanks to Archie using half of my attic as an owl roost. I really needed to clean this place up.

So, I got up and started picking up my clothes.

I'd gathered up half the clothes when I caught sight of myself in the mirror. My hair looked a mess, my face was splotchy—the way it got when I was anxious. I stared at myself, and my image stared back at me.

"I'm doing it again," I said to myself in the mirror. The redhead staring back didn't disagree "Ugh, why am I doing this again?" I threw the clothes I'd gathered down in a pile on my bed. "Maybe Emma was right a while back. Maybe I do need therapy."

"I'm divine. I think that means I can do spiritual counseling. You're doing what again?" Archie called from outside the open window. With a silent flap, he sailed inside. "What are you doing? Anything I can help with?" He settled himself on the perch my sisters made him, and tilted his head.

"Now you offer?" I snapped. "Where were you

an hour ago when I was getting fired from my job, Mr. Goddess's Own Owl?"

Archie clicked his beak. "Feeling useless since you got fired? I can totally understand that. I was thinking. You could get another job. I mean there must be something else you can do."

"There's lots of other things I can do, featherhead. I'm quite capable when I need to be." Which was probably why Rex's winning play had gotten under my skin so much. I should have seen it coming, and I didn't. I missed it. I locked eyes with the owl. "Look, I'm sorry. I didn't mean to snap at you. You know it's not really about the job, right?"

The owl nodded. "I know. I'm sorry, too," he said.

"Not your fault."

"I mean in general. I am sorry you're suffering." He leaned his head into my hand and made a purr-like sound in his throat. I gently rubbed his head and sighed.

Archie could be a sweet bird when he wanted to be.

He just rarely wanted to be.

"You know, when I was in the military," I told Archie, sitting down in the chair next to him. "I knew what the Witches' Council wanted us to do

—at least a good portion of the time—was questionable at best, completely corrupt at worst. I hated being used by them. Really hated it. I didn't sign up to be a political pawn, or a henchman. But I also just...didn't want to think about it. I couldn't. I mean, I was a soldier, right?" I felt tears coming and blinked quickly to stop them. "I couldn't leave. I couldn't affect anything. I couldn't change anything. I had no power. Even if I wanted to, I couldn't just walk out and come home."

The owl clicked his beak to acknowledge he heard me, but said nothing.

"Anyway, I'd clean when I felt frustrated, when I knew something was screwed up and I couldn't change anything. When I felt out of control." I picked up the balled clothes and held them up. "I just started doing it again."

"What feels out of control?" he asked.

"This thing with Emma and Rex...I think it's rattled me more than I want to admit." I threw the clothes back on the ground. "It's bringing up all sorts of reminders of what my life used to be like. Things I'd rather not remember. If that makes any sense. Ugh, I thought I'd left this garbage behind." I self-consciously ran my hand through my short hair. "But here I am, back again, feeling like I have no power."

"People are people wherever you go, Astra, whether it's in the heavens or the mortal realm. You can change your situation, but you can't change the nature of all those who live in that situation with us," Archie told me, his big eyes sympathetic. "Who controls your world and your life?"

"Well, me," I said with little conviction.

Archie frowned, his wings bent like little arms."Now, that wasn't an answer to inspire confidence. Who controls you?"

I looked hard at the owl. "I do," I said, my voice stronger.

He looked pleased. "That's my girl. Say that to yourself in the mirror. You control yourself." Archie nodded. "Besides, you're not powerless, and the fact that you think you are shows how little the reality in your head matches the reality in your life. Power literally sparks from your fingertips, woman."

I held up my hands and looked at them. "You know what this is, don't you?"

"You're changing the subject. I was giving a truly inspired pep talk, you know. But yes, I know that electricity is power, and those are sparks. Yeah?" The owl stepped to a low branch, his head tilted to the side. His feathers were ruffled from preening. "How much more do you want me to tell you about it? You can, with all you know, put everything together." The pointed tufts on his head jutted straight up. "I'm not a cheat sheet, you know."

"How about I just grab a feather off your butt and read you?" I asked him with a half-smile. "Sift through the images, see what you've seen." I wiggled my bare fingers at him. "Uncover all your buried secrets."

"You don't want to do that," he warned, quickly hopping to a higher branch out of my reach. "First, you might not be able to handle it. This noggin contains a lot of memories." He waved his wing wildly. "Second, my secrets are buried in the backyard. If Ami ever finds out how many of the rabbits I've eaten?" His feathers shook. "I'll never hear the end of it."

I chuckled.

Archie's peppy banter managed to pull me out of the funk I'd started to slide into.

Which, to be honest, was probably the point.

"Okay, let's focus on Will Fisher," I told the goddess's own owl. I held out my arm, he hopped on, and we headed downstairs to see if Ami discovered anything. I also needed to check in with Ayla and her ghost spy brigade. "I need to stop thinking about that stupid vampire."

"Right," Archie said. "I agree. Focus. And not on the vampire."

We bumped into Althea on the second floor landing.

And I do mean bumped. She nearly walked into us while mumbling some potion recipe to herself, stopping at the last moment with a lurch. "Sorry! Distracted. What are you guys doing?"

"Stopping a death!" Archie told Althea proudly. "We are focused! We are ready to rumble!"

"How's the potion coming?" I asked.

Archie gave me a withering look. "Great job on not thinking about the bloodsucker, there, Astra."

"So, I've got a good portion of it worked out." Althea wore a dark smock, her hair in a tight bun tied with a black bandanna. A sparkling pink powder smear glowed from her nose. "I ran into a problem, though. I don't think I can make it work without vampire blood."

"I know a few vampires from back in the day," I said, thinking. "I could call and find—"

"I don't think you're getting my meaning here, big sister." Althea held up her hands. "Emma," she said, waving her right hand. "Rex the vampire," she said, waving her left hand in the air. She linked them together by interlocking her fingers, then tugged the link apart to break the chain. "That only happens with vampire blood," she said finally, holding the left hand out. "I don't need some random vampire's blood. I need Rex's blood. Because his blood is what I need to get out of Emma's blood to break the bond." Her glasses were low on her nose, and she peered over the top rims at us. "Get it now?"

"I'll get it," I told her without elaborating. "I can get it tonight."

Althea stared at me. "You get it, or you'll get it?"

"I'll get the blood."

"It'll be dark by then, though," Althea said as if that changed everything.

"So?"

"So he's a freaking vampire, Astra. They're super powerful at night. Are you crazy?"

"Nope. I'm not."

My sister looked at me like she was

questioning my sanity. "I think I'm starting to get why Mom has some concerns about you."

Archie, riding on my shoulder, let out what sounded like a chuckle.

"You'll be here, won't you?" I asked. "Trust me. I'll get it."

"I'll be here." Althea sounded doubtful. "I just don't know if you'll be here. Mom is going to ground me until I'm thirty if you wind up getting turned into a vampire. I don't want a vampire for a sister," she warned me. Suddenly, her face fell. "Oh, man, don't tell Emma I said that. I wouldn't want to hurt her feelings."

I wondered if I would ever get the chance to tell Emma anything anymore. "I won't. But don't worry, I'll be fine. I'm always fine."

"Sure. You say that. One day, though, that luck you have? It's going to run out." Althea glanced at a book on a side table in the hallway. I followed her gaze and realized it was open to a page with a black-and-white photo of a cheerful young woman. "Wow. Is that you?"

With a start I realized it *was* me, in high school. Someone had been looking at my yearbook. "Yeah, that's me. A long time ago. Fifteen years, I guess?"

Out of seemingly nowhere, Althea asked,

"What did you mean when you said you were back again to feeling like you had no power?" She had such intent in her eyes when she asked it. Althea always seemed to know what she was after.

I narrowed my eyes. "Were you eavesdropping?"

"You have no door to your entire floor, Astra. And you're kind of loud."

You have a door, dear sister. "I was a real jerk when I was in the military, though I didn't really know it," I admitted without embarrassment. "I ignored things I shouldn't have, and when I did notice problems? I deliberately pushed them away so I wouldn't have to think about them."

"Why?"

Oh, kiddo, the answer to that question might take days. "Because it was the job. I had my orders. To cut myself slack, I was taken advantage of—like a lot of other people. But I hurt people that didn't deserve to be hurt." Althea stared at me intently as she listened to my words. I couldn't tell what she was thinking. "I'm not that person anymore. I wouldn't let that happen to me again." I paused, and thought about what I said. "Well, I'm less that person than I used to be. Let's put it that way."

"What happened to change your mind?" she asked curiously.

"I don't know. Maybe it was the defeat of the Witches' Council," I told her. "Maybe I just finally admitted to myself that there was no greater purpose to what I was assigned to do. Maybe I came home and realized that there could be something more to my life than the military. Maybe Emma helped me to—" I stopped. "Anyway, I finally realized the things I did weren't who I was. There's always some kind of opportunity or lesson or reward for correcting your course when you screw up, Althea. If we pay attention, if we're open to the possibilities, we can change. But that doesn't mean it's easy."

"That was kind of profound, Astra," Althea said with a smile. "You kind of sounded like Mom for a minute."

Oh, dear goddess, no.

I did not.

Nope.

"Just remember, sis, you never stop being who you are," I said. "You stay true to yourself, or you betray yourself. Those are your choices in life. And when you betray yourself?" I raised my eyebrow. "It can get hard to live with, and be hard to come back from."

"Yeah," Archie said. "Like with the rabbits in the back yard. To not eat them? That would be a betrayal of who I am. Total betrayal! I'd need therapy." The owl whacked me in the head with his wing. "Maybe you should go have this conversation with your sister Ami. It might get her off my back."

AYLA SIGHED. "I'm sorry, Astra, but the ghosts won't tell us."

Not only was I dealing with a stubborn glass ashtray that wouldn't let me read its memories, but now we had ghost spies that felt it was better to withhold information. Could I possibly get a break here? "What does that mean?"

"I don't know," she said with a shrug. "But I'm sure they'll tell us when we need to know."

"Did they say anything about the guy's location? I mean, is he close by?"

"Yeah, I guess so," Ayla said, shrugging again like she'd forgotten to DVR a soap opera for me. "I mean, these are Forkbridge ghosts, so I guess he's in town? They seem to know something, but they're being all cagey and cryptic and stuff.

Which, I mean, they are ghosts. It's not that out of the ordinary for them. You know?"

"No," I said flatly. "I don't know."

Ayla shook her head, her back ramrod straight. "Look, they don't know. Or won't tell us. Or don't want us to know. I'm sorry, Astra," Ayla said. "I wish I had better news for you. They seem much more concerned about the fight between you and Rex, if you want to know the truth. They think you should go deal with that before dealing with this other stuff."

I didn't like the way Ayla said that. It made it sound like an explanation—a reason the ghosts were withholding Will Fisher's location.

"Ayla, can you tell me exactly—word for word —what the ghosts said to you about Will Fisher?" I asked as clearly and precisely as I could manage. "I need to know whether we can get any data from them at all, or if we should just write them off as a source of information."

She swallowed hard and fidgeted. Suddenly, Ayla looked unsure of herself.

I could guess why. If the ghosts weren't going to participate in the case, that meant Ayla's participation in the investigation would have a pretty limited scope—and she knew it. Her only other talent—translocation—was very much a one and done kind of power. If we need something moved, she could move it. End of involvement.

"The ghosts aren't lying, if that's what you're saying," Ayla said.

"I didn't say they were lying," I told her, surprised. "I just don't understand if the ghosts you talked to are just not being helpful, or if there's something else going on here?"

"I told you. They want you to deal with the Rex thing first," Ayla said again.

"What does that even mean, deal with the Rex thing first?"

My mother walked into the room, and before even asking any questions, she frowned at me. "Astra, stop badgering Ayla," my mother told me. "I'm sure she's told you everything she knows as well as she understood it."

What the heck? Ayla was thirteen, not three. "I'm not badgering her. She's the one that wanted to help." I glared at my mother. "I'm trying to understand her answers. They're not making sense."

"They make perfect sense!" Ayla told me. "They think Astra's not going to get anything done unless she fixes whatever's going on with her and Rex! I keep saying that! She's just not listening."

I...wait...what?

"There you go, Astra," my mother said. "Now stop all the bickering, I'm not in the mood for it. I know you lost your job today, but that's no reason to take it out on your sisters."

I whirled around to face my mother. "I'm not taking anything out on anyone! And by the way, I'm not in the mood to race out the door and save Will Fisher, alcoholic insurance salesman, either, Ma, but I don't exactly get a choice in the matter, do I?"

"Astra," my mother said, raising her voice. "We're not going to start this again, are we?"

"If you all could stop bickering with each other," my Aunt Gwennie said as she walked in with Ami, "we may have a lead on Will Fisher."

Ami held up her phone. "He's just been arrested for stealing a million-dollar painting from Bath Studios in Orlando. Ami turned and looked at me. "By Emma."

"So, if you're looking for him, I think jail may be a good place to start."

CHAPTER FIVE

I dialed Detective Sullivan's number, and she answered on the first ring.

"Hey, Astra, what's up?" Emma's voice sounded falsely cheerful—like she was deliberately distancing this new conversation from everything that happened in the morning. "I'm a little busy, so if you have a question, make it quick. I just arrested some insurance dude for stealing a painting, and I don't know where the painting is." She lowered her voice. "You would have been instrumental on this case."

"You're right. I would have been," I retorted. I felt relieved. Relieved that she picked up the phone, relieved that the two of us were still chatty with each other. "I'm actually calling about that guy. Will Fisher?"

She paused in surprise and then said, "Yep, that's his name." There was a long silence on the other end. Then, "I don't even know if I want to know the answer to this, but how did you know? About Fisher, I mean."

"It actually hit the news already, for one. But… yeah, I knew about it, or him, before that. I need —" I paused. "I need to talk with you. Will's life is in danger." I paused again for emphasis. "You know, the sparkly kind of danger? The glow kind of danger? The bright lights of—"

"Card?" she asked quickly.

"Yep."

It sounded like Emma covered the phone, and I heard a muffled conversation with someone. Then she came back on the line with me and whispered, "You think he's innocent?"

"I didn't say that. I know little more than what I've told you. I don't know whether he's innocent, guilty, or whatever. All I know is someone might want him dead, and a certain other person wants him alive. Beyond that, I've got very little to go on other than feelings and suspicions."

"Okay." She sounded frustrated. "You're not an employee of the police department anymore,

Astra. I'm not supposed to give you any special access to information. So, I don't even know how we do this. Or if we even can." She cursed Rex under her breath, and I refrained from openly agreeing with her that he was an utter pain in the keister. It wasn't the time.

"I get it. That's going to make what we both have to do a lot more complicated, don't you think?"

"Well, right now, he's in lockup being processed in. Will, not Rex."

Oh, if only, I thought. "I get it."

"Since this isn't a violent crime, he'll probably get bail. Give me a second. Let me look at the schedule." I heard Emma tapping on her computer. "It looks like the town justice has a spot open in an hour and a half. At four. If I had to guess, since there's nothing much going on, he'll slide into that spot and get sprung soon after. His lawyer's already here."

So Will Fisher will get out of jail only a few hours before Rex emerges from whatever underground lair he hides in all day. That would make my planned confrontation of the stupid vampire inconvenient. "If he gets out, he might be killed. He's safer in jail, isn't he?"

"Not necessarily. But whether he is or he isn't?

Nothing I can do. I have no legitimate argument to give the prosecutor to keep him locked up."

I was quiet a moment, thinking. "Look, can we meet somewhere? Share information before he gets out?"

"I'm kind of busy. I can't really get away," she said. "Oh, wait! I know! I'm going over to Right Way Storage to go through some of the guy's stuff. They already looked through it for any stolen art. I just need to go through it and see if there's anything else. It'll just be me. Can you meet me there?"

I looked at the time on my phone. "Yeah." It was a risk, but it would work. "You sure you won't get in trouble?"

"Not if we bump into each either while you're shopping for a storage unit, right? Okay, I'll give you the address, just—" Emma paused for a moment. "Hang on, the Captain wants to ask me something."

I heard the muffled buzz of a conversation on the other end of the phone, and then someone was speaking to me directly.

"Astra, you're not an employee of the police department anymore," he told me sternly.

"Yes, Captain, the letter you guys hustled over before the ink was dry made that perfectly clear.

I'm not an employee of the police department anymore." I said firmly. "I understand the situation. I'm just talking to my friend, Emma. It's a personal call, sir. Totally a personal call."

"We can't have you showing up at crime scenes," he added—without explicitly telling me not to.

I took the loophole and ran with it. "I understand, Captain," I told him.

"You and Emma are just talking as friends," he said. "We're not telling you anything about anything you don't already know. We're not sharing anything directly with you. And I'm telling you, if you somehow find out information you're not supposed to have, Astra, I will assume that you either eavesdropped on private conversations or used your powers to spy on them. And if you spy on the case, I will expect you to turn over any and all relevant information to Emma immediately." Captain Harmon cleared his throat. "Are we clear?"

I blinked. Did Captain Harmon just say what I think he said?

I do believe the captain just found a way to have the best of both worlds.

He has a psychic on the payroll without…paying.

"Thank you, sir. That's very clear," I said with as much politeness as I could muster.

I could hear Emma coughing as if trying to cover a laugh. "Right, then," Captain Harmon said. "As long as you are not doing police work. I'll put Emma back on now. Oh, and if anyone asks?" The captain paused for a second. "You were once an employee. You're not anymore."

"I understand. I'll be careful." What better cover story was there than what was already true?

"Be careful of what? Nothing to be careful of," he said gruffly. "And again, I'm sorry about all this."

Emma's voice came back on the line. "Okay, on to business. I just texted you the address of the storage facility. Like I said, I'm going to go through his stuff again, but I have no idea what I'm looking for. So we can talk there."

I DROVE up in my Jeep just as Emma was pulling up in her car. Her Chevy Malibu looked as old and beat-up as ever, but I knew it could overtake any vehicle it needed to chase. "Hey," I greeted her as we met one another in the parking lot. "To tell you the truth, I didn't think we'd be back here doing something like this so soon."

"Yeah, I was gonna come over today and talk to you about what happened. Rex didn't even tell me he was filing a complaint against you last night," Emma said with frustration. "Nothing like finding out your brother screwed with your friend and your career at a time when you can't even go have a conversation with him. I think he does that on purpose." She glanced off into the distance as if she was searching the horizon for the vampire. "I didn't see this coming."

"I didn't, either. And I don't blame you, Emma. I get that he's trying to protect you. Still, I think his vampire nature has warped his idea of what actions are appropriate and what are not in this situation," I told her.

For a moment, I thought about telling her I'd asked Althea to come up with a potion to break the blood bond with her brother, but anything Emma could hear, Rex could also hear. I didn't want to put my sister in danger, and I didn't want to give the vampire heads-up about what I was planning.

"Maybe." Emma stood, tense, looking at me. "I'm really sorry about all this, Astra."

"Again, not your fault. He really stepped over

the line getting me fired, though. Especially getting me fired with a lie."

"Gosh, Astra, are you telling me you wouldn't want to date my brother?" Emma joked with a smile. After what Rex pulled, she seemed far less concerned about what he overheard and what he didn't.

That, at least, was an improvement.

"Do I want to date the guy that brought down my career with a falsified report?" I raised my eyebrow. "No, Emma, I have no interest in your brother beyond potentially sticking him in the chest with a pointy stick."

"You're just joking about that, right?" She smiled at me.

I smiled back but didn't answer.

"Okay, wait. You wouldn't actually kill Rex, would you?" she asked, her tone suddenly nervous. "Look, Astra, I know he's acting like a complete jerk right now, but my brother is in there somewhere. I just know he is. It'll be hard for you to believe, but when he was alive? He was a really great guy. He really was."

The Florida afternoon storm clouds rolled in, and it began raining. Emma and I stood under the eaves watching people in the shopping center next door scramble into their vehicles.

Finally, I turned to her in the rain and touched her arm. "I know you love your brother, Emma. I'm not going to hurt him, at least not unprovoked. Not because I agree with you that he was a really great guy, but because I don't want to hurt you." I made a sour face. "You know, the way he keeps doing."

She gave me a look but didn't respond.

"I didn't know, after your phone call, if you and I were going to be friends anymore," I said. Emma looked at me, surprise on her face. I shrugged. "Well, think about it. Rex was pretty smart to attack my position in the police department. Our friendship developed because we spent so much time together on the job. Its foundation, really, was in work."

"Well, sure, Astra, but that's not all our friendship is," Emma pointed out.

"No?" I looked her in the eye. "Honestly, I wasn't sure."

"That's because you just got out of the military. I've been out a lot longer than you. I know it seems like you're instant best friends with whoever's in your squad, right? And then you get transferred, or they get transferred, and you semi-keep in contact with a few—but with most? You don't. Oh, sure, you don't care about them any less, but still. It's kind of a transactional friendship, right?"

I nodded. "I guess."

"That's not us, Astra. I don't know the families of the soldiers in my platoon, even today. Don't know their sisters or their mother or their crazy aunt with the flowers." Emma nodded, her expression serious. "I love my brother, Astra, and I get where he's coming from with this, but it doesn't change that you're my best friend." She laughed sharply. "And I'm a female detective in Florida. I'm ex-military. If you think I find it easy to make female friends? You're out of your mind."

Since getting the call about Rex's report, I'd been out of sorts. My powers were unreliable. I was fidgety and nervous when I was ordinarily steady. Rex's move against me had rattled me, and its success bothered me more than I wanted to admit. But the potential loss of Emma from my life?

That rattled me most of all.

I felt the tension draining from my body as she spoke, a tension I didn't even realize I'd been feeling.

I didn't want Emma to choose between Rex and me, but I suspected if she got to that point, I would be the person to lose. She would choose her brother—and I would never blame her for it. Emma and I had only known each other for a few months. Maybe we'd attempt to keep in touch, but then we'd drift away until there was no relationship at all.

As that possibility faded, I felt less scattered.

"I really appreciate you saying that," I told her. "I feel the same way. I know I can't get my job back, but I don't want to lose you as a friend. Unfortunately, there's very few people that get me, either."

"How many people would understand a best friend that drags an owl around?" Emma joked. "I mean, seriously?"

We both laughed.

"Look, I know we have a lot going on," Emma said, "but I really need to search that storage unit. We can talk about the case there. Honestly, I'm really surprised a Star card flipped over for this guy." Emma moved toward the storage company's office. "He doesn't seem like the type of guy a goddess would want to save."

I OPENED the storage unit door and flashed my flashlight inside. It was small, maybe ten feet by ten, and had seen better days—both the building walls and the contents within it. Not a place I would hide a million-dollar painting, that's for sure. Instead, there was a beat-up couch, a lamp, and a kitchen chair—and a pile of something in the corner.

Scanning the scratched-up wall, I found a light switch (I hoped) and flipped it up. A moment passed, and the room was awash in the light of a single bulb.

Which only made the place look more creepy, if you want to know the truth.

"What's that?" Emma asked, nodding toward the pile.

"Don't know. Can't tell from here."

We walked carefully over and looked down. There were clothes, magazines, and an old TV on its side. There was a thin, undisturbed film of dust on everything. It looked like it hadn't been touched. "I thought you said officers already went through this storage unit?" I asked Emma.

"I did. I mean, I was told they'd already searched the place." She looked around. "This is weird," Emma said. "I think we should get back up. This whole place needs to be searched again." Emma frowned. "If someone has even searched it, which, looking at it? I would put money on the fact that nobody's been here." She pulled out her phone to call the captain.

"Wait a sec. We're already here. We can look first," I said. "Besides," I said, holding up my hand, "if there is something here that's useful, I can get to it before forensics puts it into evidence."

"How could they have missed this?" Emma said.

I followed her eyes. "What? How could they have missed what? You find something?"

"This. This whole storage unit. I suspect the guy of stealing art, and he has a storage unit in his name. Right? Searching the storage unit? That would kinda be a top priority after his house, wouldn't you think?" Emma looked frustrated. "And me being a detective, I would think the storage unit would be the more likely location for the stolen art than the house, right?" I nodded. "So, tell me how the police department just completely misses searching this?"

"It does seem rather unlikely," I agreed as I picked up a painting. "Is this stolen?"

Emma made a face. "Goodness, no. That's a framed poster from Walmart or something. You know nothing about art, do you?"

"I know art consists of pictures in frames." I

held up the image of an apple. "This is a picture in a frame."

"Art needs to be wrapped, protected. Stored at a specific temperature when possible." Her head swung around. "This doesn't look like some highly organized place to keep stolen art before it gets fenced. Instead, this looks like a bunch of stuff Will's mother gave him that his wife didn't want in the house, but he couldn't bring himself to throw away."

I chuckled. "I met his wife," I told Emma. "Your guess tracks more than you know."

"Oh? I haven't met her yet. Tell me about her."

"Ami could probably tell you a lot more than I can. My sister did the reading for her where the Star card came up." I picked up one item after another with my gloved hand, examined it, and then discarded it into a pile. "There were a few things that stuck out. One, she thinks her husband is an alcoholic. They've been married for twenty-three years, and she came in for a psychic reading for what I suspect was the first time in her life. She sounded like she'd reached the end of her rope and was looking for guidance about what to do." I put my hand on my hip. "Of course, the creepy glowing card came up, we asked a few questions, and she ran out of the store in a panic because, you know, the paranormal and all."

"You guys really need to come up with a better shtick for when that happens," Emma said. "What was she at the end of her rope about?"

"Yeah, Ami said the same thing this morning. As for ropes ending, she didn't really say specifically. I went over to the Barber Insurance Agency this morning to try and get more info, and is that a weird place—"

"You went over there?" Emma asked, her eyes wide. "Will is suspected of insurance fraud, Astra. That office may be filled with criminals, possibly violent ones. Why didn't you call me before you took a risk like that?"

"Well, one, I was just looking for a guy that I'm supposed to keep from dying, so that's why I went over there. Two, I did call you. I called you, like, three times. You didn't call me back. I guess you were too busy organizing my dismissal from the Forkbridge Police Department?" I told her with a raised eyebrow. "And three, I didn't know anything about a stolen painting or possible insurance fraud or Will being arrested when I went."

"Because I didn't pick up the phone," Emma nodded.

"Well, I'm not blaming you for the unwarranted risks that I took, but yes—"

"Okay, okay, I get it. Let's just skip over the witty banter and sarcastic zingers. Did you find anything out?"

"I talked to a guy named Charles Fisher—who swears up, down, left, right, and sideways that he is not the brother of Will Fisher. There was some female in the back office I never saw, but when I came in, the two seemed deep in conversation."

Emma was taking notes in her notepad. "Got it. What was weird about the place?"

"It just didn't look…I don't know, legit? There were posters on the walls with push pins. They still smoked in there like it was still the fifties which…I mean, who smokes in an office where you bring clients nowadays? The office itself wasn't marked very well. The windows were mirrored, so you couldn't see in. The phone didn't ring. There were no clients in there. The whole thing just felt like—"

"Like a front?" Emma offered.

"Yeah, maybe." I looked around the storage unit. "Okay, go ahead and call the captain. Er, the chief. Wait a minute." I looked up. "Is he the police chief or the police captain?"

"He's both. Since he supervises the police

station, he is the captain. Since there is only one police station in Forkbridge, he's also the chief of police." Emma shrugs. "I call him chief or captain, depending on what I want from him."

While Emma called Captain Harmon, I examined the couch and chair one more time in case I'd missed a hidden compartment. Which, you know, I hadn't.

Just a beat-up couch and chair.

After a quick conversation, she hung up. "We're in the wrong—or the right—storage unit."

"What does that mean?"

"This is the one the guy at the reception desk said belongs to Will Fisher. But the captain just told me the forensics team searched another storage unit on the other side of the property. That's the one the insurance company told us about." She put her hand on her waist. "And you'll never guess the name of the insurance company."

CHAPTER SIX

$\mathcal{W}$e were barely in the second storage unit for twenty minutes. It had clearly been picked over or—possibly—never held anything to begin with. There was nothing to examine, nothing to look at. Emma wanted to ask Will Fisher why he rented two different storage units despite neither of them being full, so we decided I'd follow Emma back toward the police station.

I slid into my Jeep, leaned over, and tossed my bag on the passenger side floorboards, and laughed. This morning, it seemed like everything was falling apart. This afternoon, I was driving back to the police station as if nothing had changed.

Well, something had changed.

I wasn't getting paid for this little trip.

Emotionally, I felt more centered than I had just a few hours ago. It was disconcerting to realize the view I had of myself—a tough lone wolf who needed nothing and no one—might not be precisely accurate anymore.

Fearing Emma might disappear from my life had been a difficult thing to face. It made me feel out of sorts, uncomfortable. A discomfort that disappeared instantly once she and I began working this case together.

Well, maybe "working" is a stretch.

Again, thanks to Rex, I wouldn't see a paycheck for this.

I pulled out of the parking lot and followed Emma as we merged onto the highway. Once I had the cruise control engaged, the phone rang.

I tapped the screen. "Hello?"

"So, maybe I'm crazy, but I have this weird feeling the thing between you and Rex isn't over," Emma said. "Forget that he's my brother for a minute. I know that he got you fired, and it's clear that you guys have problems with each other—"

"Problems with each other, Emma?" I laughed. "That might be the understatement of the year."

"You know when I first asked him about you?

It sounded like he really had respect for you. Rex told me he knew a couple of vampires that you'd arrested, and you'd brought them in unharmed."

"Certainly possible. Vampires tended to run. And, of course, they were brought in unharmed. We weren't an execution squad."

"Maybe you weren't. Rex claimed a lot of your fugitive coworkers pushed it way too far. They'd just whack a fugitive vamp with a wooden stick, suck them up with a wet-dry vac, and bring them back to Impy," Emma said.

"I highly doubt that," I told her dryly.

"But would you know if it was happening?" Her voice sounded sure and steady again, as Rex's act and my getting fired had set her thinking off in a direction that produced less anxiety than before. "At first, after I woke up? He was really enthusiastic about you. Said he liked working with you, that you're brilliant."

"Well, I am brilliant. But none of what you're saying makes any sense if you consider how he's treated me since then," I pointed out. "I mean, he got me fired, Emma. That's not something you do to someone you respect."

"That's what I'm saying, Astra. Something changed. Something changed after I woke up. I don't think I realized it until today, until he took the step he did. But something that night at your mother's house? His whole attitude toward you, toward your family? It changed."

I thought about it. "Maybe."

"I know my brother has his faults. He had them as a human. I'm sure he has even more as a vampire. But Rex has never been dishonest, not that I know of—"

I chuckled. "Emma, I need to point out something about your brother that you may have forgotten. As a vampire, he worked for the mob. By definition, that's a pretty dishonest job."

"Rex said that by the time he joined up, there was an internal fight going on. So, for the most part, they weren't doing a lot of…organized crime-type things," Emma responded.

I was glad the phone's microphone wasn't sensitive enough to pick up my exasperated sigh. I loved Emma, and she was a smart cookie, but I'd never seen anyone make so many excuses for someone in my life.

When I didn't respond, she asked, "Astra, did I lose you?"

"Just with your observation," I said quietly, hopefully too quiet for her to hear. "I'd also like to point out that your ex-mafia brother just came up with the money to buy a warehouse he's converting to a club. What did he do, cash in his bitcoin?" Before she could answer, I added, "You know, I'm less concerned about what changed in Rex than what's changed in you. Where is all this coming from?"

A short pause. "What do you mean? All what?"

"This sudden desire to discuss and figure out what's going on between Rex and me. I mean, this has been going on for a month already. For most of that month, you didn't speak to me about it and, what's more, you treated me like garbage—"

"I did not!"

"—to satisfy Rex's paranoia. Not dealing with those issues culminated in my getting fired for sexually harassing your vampire brother. You've been avoiding the subject with me for a whole moon cycle now—"

"Normal people say a month, Astra," Emma said tartly.

"—and now, suddenly, you want to work through it." The highway wound its way through long stretches of empty swampland, enough of a stretch that various bugs splattered themselves against my windshield in a patchwork design of insect slaughter. No wonder Florida had so many frogs. The air was a smorgasbord of bug plenty. "I get him—sort of. Your brother holds me responsible for what the pixies did to you. It's almost understandable, you know?"

"That's what I'm saying, Astra. I don't think it's that simple. Before he got here, before that happened? He didn't tell me to stay away from you. He even told me a couple of times that if I needed to, you could probably be trusted. Suddenly, almost overnight, that all changed. And that changed the night of the dinner, not right when I woke up."

"Have you asked him?" I asked her. "Have you just straight out asked your brother what the deal is? Why he changed his mind about me?"

I followed Emma to the exit and turned right. The police station was just a minute away.

"I have. Of course, I have," she told me, her tone somewhat annoyed. "That doesn't mean I've gotten an answer, though. He just keeps repeating that he's concerned for my safety and that you and your family are too dangerous for me to have contact with. But he never says why, and he never tells me why his opinion changed."

I didn't know what to tell her, so I just apologized. "I'm really sorry you have to go through this, Emma."

"Did something happened back at Impy that

he could've found out about? Something you did, maybe, that freaked him out?"

"I beg your pardon?" I parked my Jeep next to her Malibu, shutting off the car and disconnecting the phone call. As we both got out of our vehicles, I called over her roof, "You want to make that sound like less of an accusation against me, maybe? I've already been accused of something once today. One a day is my limit here."

Emma glanced at Jared Upton, the sixty-two-year-old forensic investigator. He had been walking by toward the station entrance—but at the sound of our voices, he stopped, turned, and stared at both of us. The rumors he's heard already today sparkled in his curious eyes.

"Jared," Emma said casually.

"Emma," he responded.

We waited, silently, for Jared to continue on his way.

He didn't.

"We can talk about this later," I told her.

Emma nodded.

Jared looked disappointed.

WE WALKED into the police station together—even though that, in and of itself, was likely to cause a little bit of a stir. I would like to say Captain Harmon looked surprised to see me, but he really didn't.

Not even a little.

"Hey, Captain!" I called loudly.

He stared.

I waved cheerfully.

He narrowed his eyes and turned away.

"Captain Harmon doesn't seem very happy to see me," I told Emma as we made our way toward her desk. "It's almost like he fired me."

The detectives' area was in the back of the central office, past a row of desks and cubicles. Halfway across the room, I spotted a woman I didn't recognize, already in Emma's chair as if she owned the place. Her hair was pulled back in a ponytail, her gem-encrusted glasses a dark pink color.

"Hi, there!" Emma chirped.

She glanced up from stacks of paperwork briefly, her coffee-brown eyes sharp and focused, but then she dropped her gaze to the desk once again.

"Rude," Emma murmured to me. Raising her

voice, she asked, "Excuse me, that's my desk. Who said you could sit here?"

A man came out of the hallway, made a beeline for the pink glasses woman, and stood behind her silently. Without saying anything to Emma and me at all, he leaned over with his arm resting on the back of her chair.

"Excuse me?" Emma said again, this time more insistent.

The man looked up.

He was wearing a suit, a black suit with a blue vest that matched his eyes. In contrast to the woman in front of him (whose attire screamed affordable), his entire get-up was clearly expensive. The shoes alone looked like they'd cost most people a month's salary. They were dark shoes with soft leather that would scuff easily if he ever did anything other than casually stroll through life.

I stared back with shock.

I knew him. Where did I know this guy from?

"Astra?" The man smiled.

My eyes snapped open. It can't be. "What on earth are you doing here?"

Moneybucks Magee stepped forward to shake my hand. "I'm Will Fisher's lawyer. I bet you're surprised to see me here."

"That's impossible," I said, giving voice to the words running through my head. "You're not a lawyer. You're a—" I snapped my mouth shut before I could utter the word *witch* out loud.

Since I come home, I'd been surprised a few times, but seeing another witch from Imperatorial City posing as an attorney in my small-town Florida home? This surprise might rank up there with being given an owl from a Greek goddess for my birthday.

And not just any witch.

One of the witches closest to the Witches' Council.

The very corrupt, ruthless, very deposed Witches' Council.

Emma studied the two of us briefly, trying to figure out what was going on. "Someone want to clue me in here?" she asked once she realized no one was going to volunteer any information.

"Astra and I have been previously acquainted, Detective," he said, extending his hand to Emma. He spoke in a low, calm voice, His black hair was longish and smooth with thick waves that had to contain buckets of volumizing mousse to get that kind of bounce. His eyes were a pale blue, the color of blue selenite.

Or his ice-cold ruthless heart.

One of the two.

Emma reached out to shake his hand as he introduced himself to her. "My name is Amadeus Bozeman."

Emma burst out laughing. "Oh, it is not. That sounds like something out of a bad romance novel or a porno." She bit back her laughter, but when he did not respond in kind, the detective blushed with embarrassment. "Wait, is it? Really? That's your name? Seriously?"

"That's really his name," I told her, my eyes narrowing. "I'm going to ask you again. What are you doing here?"

Amadeus glanced around the station. "I told you, but if you want more than that, Astra—considering our history—we probably shouldn't talk right here." He motioned toward one of the interview rooms. "We should go somewhere else a bit more private. Detective Sullivan, I trust you can help Melinda Barber?" Amadeus gestured toward the nervous woman still buried in paperwork at Emma's desk. She was seemingly oblivious to our discussion.

Barber?

As in the Barber Insurance Agency?

"Sure, I can do that," Emma agreed a little too eagerly, pointing toward the free interrogation room. "You two go right in there and talk. Totally private. It's perfect."

Uh-huh. Like that was going to happen.

"That's an interview room, Amadeus," I told him. "They have one-way windows and microphones in them." He looked confused. "So police and prosecutors can listen to and watch the conversation without being seen or heard?" Whatever magic Amadeus conjured to procure a license to practice law, it didn't appear to transfer any actual knowledge with it.

"Right." Amadeus glanced around. "Come on, then," he said as he reached for my hand. "Let's take a walk."

Just before he could grab it, I stepped back.

Amadeus seemed surprised at my reaction, but he didn't push it. He even apologized with a curt, "Sorry." The witch walked toward the front door, glancing behind him only once to make sure I was following.

Amadeus Bozeman.

Here.

Why on earth was that man in this town?

And why was he claiming to be Will Fisher's lawyer?

WE WALKED out of the police station together, passing police giving us little more than a curious side glance. Following, I caught the scent of his cologne on a warm breeze and chuckled quietly.

He even smelled expensive, like unearned money.

We walked the sidewalk in silence for half a block. Finally putting enough distance between us and everyone else, Amadeus Bozeman turned toward me and said, "I heard you were here. I didn't expect to run into you so soon."

"I'm here because my family's from here. Why I'm here isn't a mystery. It's even pretty expected, considering my mom's universally known location as Athena's priestess," I said. I looked up at him, the relentless sun behind him almost blinding me. "You, on the other hand, have no business here. What the hell are you doing here posing as an attorney?" I asked. When he didn't answer, I added, "What is your game, Amadeus?"

He smiled as if he expected my antagonistic words. "Same old Astra, suspicious of everyone. And for your information, I'm not posing as an attorney. I am an attorney. No amount of poking into my past or examining documents or calling law schools would give any indication otherwise," Amadeus told me confidently. "To be perfectly honest, I do have a game. But it has nothing to do with you."

I was suddenly wary.

It was like the pixie problem all over again.

In the last case, it looked like a typical rich person murdered for money thing. (Well, the case looked like it was to prevent a rich person being murdered for money.) Looked that way for a while. But I made a little bit of progress on a perfect, totally normal human case, and wham!

A pixie. And then another. And then a whole freaking pixie clan.

Now, this case? I felt like I whammed into a witch.

The cases without paranormals were so much easier.

I had one.

One.

It was easier.

"Okay, let's pretend I believe you about the lawyer thing. Why are you representing Will Fisher?" I asked. "How are you involved in this stolen artwork thing or with that insurance company?"

"Stolen artwork?" Amadeus asked politely.

"Wow, you're really on the ball as a lawyer, huh? The guy you're representing was arrested for something you're going to play dumb about?"

"Now, now, Astra, there's no need to be hostile," Amadeus said smoothly, with a small smile. "We're old friends, you and I."

We were not old friends. Amadeus Bozeman wouldn't have wasted air saying hello in the Ministry's hallway when passing by me. He was way above my pay grade, and as far as he was concerned back then, I was well below his. We knew of each other.

But we were not friends.

"I visited the agency this morning, and, frankly, they didn't look like they could afford the down payment on a pair of your shoes. Nothing about the place screamed 'fine art' insurers." I narrowed my eyes. "And isn't it a conflict of interest to be here with the owner of an insurance company Will Fisher works for while representing him? I assume they're the ones that insured the painting everyone is looking for, right?" I asked, taking a shot in the dark as to who Miranda Barber was.

"You've been to the Barber office?" Amadeus asked, his face flashing concern for just a tiny moment.

"I have. Why do you care?"

"No reason," Amadeus responded smoothly, his face relaxing into nonchalance. He had a way of standing so he was tilted just slightly to the right. It made him look like he was perpetually posing for a picture. "To answer your questions, since I know you won't stop asking them—I'm here because a friend extended an offer for a business opportunity. Since all of us were unceremoniously banished from Imperatorial City—oh, excuse me, Paranormopolis," he said with a slight sneer. "I've had to quickly spin up a life out here in the human world. This is just a stop on that tour."

He explained this to me with the confidence of someone used to having his words taken at face value.

"I wasn't banished," I told Amadeus. "I was fired when they dismantled half the military, but I could have stayed and gotten some pencil-pushing job. I didn't want to stay, but I could have." I tilted my head. "I take it you didn't have that option?"

"No," Amadeus responded sharply. "I was informed by that flea-bitten bear I should be grateful I wasn't imprisoned for my crimes against the paranormal world." The handsome witch's face twisted in anger. "Sanctimonious do-gooders. As if running some animal clan is even remotely comparable to running a bureaucracy responsible for all paranormal-kind. Comrade Scout doesn't have a clue what he's doing."

I guess the charm is just the top layer of a seething resentment sandwich?

Interesting. I didn't know much about Amadeus's role in Impy, just that he was close to the Witches' Council. I searched my memories for his title...Ambassador? Consort? I probably should have paid more attention in Political Paranormal class.

What I did know was that the new government banished very few people.

Those that were banished?

There was usually a pretty good reason.

"Yeah, so, I don't care," I told Amadeus, shrugging as if his crimes were meaningless. "That's all in the past. I don't want to know your sob story of what happened to you when the Witches' Council fell, Bozeman. I want to know what you're doing in my town. Right now. In the middle of a paranormal and a police case."

"Your town?" He raised a perfectly shaped eyebrow.

"I said what I said."

He stared at me as if I were lying. Or bluffing.

"I'm a lawyer and a witch. Where else would I be?" he said without actually answering the question. "Besides, there are no paranormal cases anymore, at least not right now."

I frowned. "What does that mean?"

"The new regime doesn't have a clue what rules to set on the rest of us, much less how to enforce any rules they come up with." He smiled at me. "For the moment, we have free rein to do as we please, Astra. With your skills? You could be quite useful. There's much money to be made off these humans."

"I'm already quite useful," I told him. "To the police department."

"Are you?"

He looked at me with eyes of glass. Amadeus was charming and handsome and elegant, and he exuded money. He also oozed calculation and insincerity.

"I am," I answered.

"Really? To the department that fired you this morning?"

I stared at Amadeus and didn't respond.

He didn't think he'd run into me, did he?

Big liar.

Amadeus reached out, grabbed my hand, and squeezed it gently as he looked me in the eyes as if to try and charm me one more time. I let him—even though I wanted to rip my hand from his—just so I could see what he'd say next.

"I can teach you all about your new life, this life among humans with no rules to constrain us. I can show you how to use your powers to become a real force to be reckoned with, virtually untouchable, and you can have all the money you would ever want." His face had a chameleon-like quality, shifting from angry to severe to sincere to smoldering like he was turning a dial on a radio looking for mood music.

I removed my hand. As Amadeus tried to keep his grip on it, my body started to send out a clear, low signal that I was standing a little too close to a predator.

"I've heard enough. The things that I want, Amadeus? Money can't buy." Because, to tell you the truth, I have no idea what I want.

But I wasn't telling him that.

"Fine." Amadeus stared at me as if I'd made the decision he expected, but not the decision he'd hoped for. "The vampire is going to ensure that you and his sister are, eventually, torn apart. Your work with the police department will come to an end, and you'll be alone again," he said, putting more of his hidden cards on the table. Though the smile remained on his face, I could see the muscles working in his jaw. "Rex is very determined. Are you sure you don't want to rethink my offer?"

I stared at the witch, alarm bells ringing in my head. "Your friend. The one that invited you here. It was Rex Sullivan?"

"Obviously," he answered in the affirmative—even though it wasn't evident to me at all until that moment. Maybe Emma's blind spot was contagious. Amadeus's voice was deep and held an outward note of menace. "It certainly wasn't the pixies."

Amadeus knew far more about what I'd been up to in Forkbridge than I'd realized—and Emma's brother had just escalated from a major annoyance to a threat.

CHAPTER SEVEN

Fifteen minutes later, I was sitting with Emma in the back of the police station. We found a private, out of the way, pseudo breakroom cluttered with files, magazines, forms, and old-fashioned yellow notepads. With the door leading to the hallway cracked open, I balanced on a rickety chair, trying to explain who Amadeus Bozeman is.

Well, who he was.

No.

Who he is.

Men like Amadeus Bozeman don't change.

"I mean, he was like one of the Praetorian Guards for the ruling class, Emma." She looked confused as if she were caught in a history final she hadn't studied for. "Okay, forget the Roman reference. You have to understand the Witches' Council first. These three women ran, like, everything in the paranormal world. The towns, the paranormals that lived in the human world. The military. Everything. They made rules; they judged guilt. The only thing they couldn't mess with, really, was the paranormal circuses. That stuff with the circuses, though, is a whole other bubbling cauldron."

Emma blinked. Her eyes were wide, and her mouth gaped like she didn't know whether to cry or jump into the air. "Wait a minute, back up. Circuses are paranormal? Like, magic elephants and stuff? Please tell me there are magic elephants at the circuses."

"That wasn't the point. But no. Not anymore."

Her face fell. "Bummer. Magic elephants would be seriously cool."

The detective's tension of the past month seemed to have melted away with the day's events —which, to be honest, kind of concerned me. Emma appeared comfortable being angry with her brother now. Being nice to me. All of a sudden. And all it took was me getting fired. "Would you focus, please? I know that's hard for you with everything going on—"

Well, that got her back up a little. "You know what? It's not hard at all. I'm fine. You, on the other hand, are sounding a little out there, friend."

I blinked. "I always sound out there. I mean, let's face it. Most of my explanations and solutions sound pretty out there."

"I think I know what's going on." Emma stared at me for a moment and then tilted her head to the side. "You know what I think it is?"

"I have no idea, but I'm sure you're going to tell me."

"You're waiting for the other shoe to drop. You think there's more to come. That suddenly, with the w—" Emma stopped herself and looked to the side. The door leading to the hallway was cracked open. "With the lawyer guy and his history showing up, you think this case just turned into one of sparkly paranormal relevance. Right?"

I gave her a slight nod. "You're not wrong. If I had to bet on it, probably."

The detective rolled her eyes. "You see pixies around every corner, Astra. This case is a simple theft case involving a crooked insurance agent that wanted to make a fast buck. That's it. Maybe Amadeus Bozeman is just like you—a paranormal out in the human world for the first time trying to find his place in it. It's not like you to prejudge a paranormal just because of who they are."

I tried not to take offense at that one. "It's not because of who he is. It's because of what Amadeus Bozeman's done. This isn't about him being a witch. And, by the way, your brother invited him to Forkbridge," I said, cutting to the bizarre coincidence that made me think none of this was coincidental.

"What does that have to do with anything? Maybe they knew each other in Las Vegas. Maybe Bozeman had a relationship with those other witches in Las Vegas, and that's how Rex met him. There are a million reasons they could know one another, Astra. I'm sure you know other paranormal people, right?"

I'd wanted to introduce Emma to the idea that her brother was involved with something sketchy slowly, carefully. In a way that would, hopefully, cushion the dawning awareness that her brother was a snake.

Despite having a vampire brother and a witch best friend, Emma didn't see sparkly supernatural villains everywhere. She was a pragmatist—and about her brother, a frustratingly eternal optimist. "Look, Emma, Amadeus didn't exactly hide the fact that he was here to exploit humans for money. And if your brother asked him here—"

Emma frowned. "Hold on. Are you saying my brother invited him here so the two of them could pull some scam?"

"Where did Rex get the money to buy a furniture store building?" I asked her with a pang of regret. "Suddenly, overnight, your brother has deep pockets to buy Forkbridge real estate? To hire a construction company? To start a business? You think that's accidental? Serendipity?"

Emma looked at me blankly, as if my words didn't compute.

I hesitated, watching her.

It was like there was a gigantic sieve on her head, and words about her brother and bad things he might be part of just got filtered right out before they hit her brain.

Fine.

I didn't want to ask Emma the next question, but I didn't see a way around it now.

"And another thing—I thought you said your parents believed Rex was dead? If that's the case, how come your brother felt so comfortable having his picture in the Gazette? With his real name? Aren't you guys worried that your parents would see it?"

Emma burst out laughing. "My parents don't think Rex is dead," Emma said, wiping tears from her eyes. "What a ridiculous thing to say! Where would you get an idea like that? They think he developed an allergy to the sun while in the military, that's all." Her laughter was full of joy and relief but also full of sadness. A sadness she seemed disconnected from.

I knew what she said was wrong.

Knew it.

I was sure—absolutely sure—she told me their parents believed Rex to be dead. When Emma first told me about her brother, she talked extensively about the pain she felt over Rex's disconnection from the family, the difficulty she had keeping the knowledge he was (in a way) still alive from her parents. She and Rex frequently fought about that issue. She wanted him to tell them. He refused.

"Oh. Your parents never thought Rex was dead?" I asked casually.

"Like I said, Astra, I really don't know where you got that idea from," the detective told me with finality. "And honestly, we have other things we need to be focused on right now, don't you think? Like where Will Fisher hid this missing painting. The insurance company is going to have to pay out if we don't find it."

I felt a dull sense of defeat. Rex Sullivan was using his vampire powers to rearrange his life around him—even if that meant manipulating Emma's understanding of reality. Vampires—all vampires—can hypnotize humans with a glance. The better their skill was, the more complex the changes they could convince their targets' to believe.

Emma was obviously her brother's target.

I knew that Rex was skilled—Emma had no memory of the issues she and her family had before he returned to Forkbridge. If I had to take a guess, Emma's parents had been dazzled and dizzied up and were equally enthusiastic about their son.

"Should we go talk to Will Fisher, then?" I suggested, pointing toward the door. I needed time to think through what to do, and working on the human aspect gave me that. Gave me a breather, a few minutes to sift through what I knew, and to decide how to proceed.

Or, you know, time to decide what kind of chopsticks to buy.

Chopsticks were still on the table as an option.

My instinct was buzzing at me like an annoying fly that these things happening—the Star card, the stolen painting, Rex, Amadeus, the Barber Insurance Agency—were all part of some spaghetti-mess of a conspiracy. At the very least, they had to be somewhat related. And regardless of whatever else was going on, I still had to keep Will Fisher alive.

But…I just couldn't get a handle on any of it. I didn't know where the threat was coming from. Where the epicenter of it all was. I just needed to find one thread I could pull, and I was sure it would all unravel.

"You think Amadeus will be okay with you in the room?" Emma asked, frowning. "You're not an employee anymore, so I really can't take you in there unless his lawyer says it's okay."

"Only one way to find out," I told her.

WE ENTERED THE INTERROGATION ROOM. Emma and I sat down on one side of the table, Will Fisher and his "attorney" Amadeus Bozeman on the other. Emma's face twisted into a grimace from the stench—the insurance agent smelled like a gin house.

"Will, this is a friend of mine. She's going to sit in on this interview while I question you. Do you have any problem with that? If you or your attorney object, I can ask Astra to leave," Emma said, gesturing toward me.

Will Fisher did not respond. He stared at the table in front of him with red-rimmed eyes, his handcuffed hands clasping one another.

Emma turned toward Amadeus. "Counselor, is your client all right with Astra being here? I need a definitive yes or no since she's not an employee of the police department."

Bozeman glanced back toward his client and then nodded. "We have no problem with Ms. Arden being in here for the interview. I am aware of her considerable skills, and she may be more of a help than I could've ever anticipated." Amadeus gave me an insincere smile and a wink. "Right, Astra?"

I glared back.

"I know you've already been read your rights, Will, but I'm going to go through them again one more time, just to be sure we're covered. All right, Mr. Fisher?"

Emma was handling the drunken insurance agent particularly gently. It surprised me. Emma's interviews usually resembled a freight train barreling through a car sitting on a railroad crossing. She read the suspect's rights, and he gave a slight nod to show he heard.

"What questions do you have, Detective?" Amadeus Bozeman asked her.

"The best thing your client can do to help himself is to tell us where the stolen painting is," Emma told the witch attorney. "I spoke with Ms. Barber, and that's the primary goal of the insurance agency. They just want the thing back. So, where is it?" Emma paused, but neither Fisher nor his attorney answered. "We've been to both of the storage units, and there was nothing there. We searched your house and came up empty." She turned to Will Fisher. "You tell me, Will. Where else should we look?"

"I can't help you," Will Fisher whispered. He glanced up at me, and our eyes met briefly. The fear in his stare was unmistakable. "I wish I could help you, Detective. You have no idea how much I wish I could help you. But I just can't. I just can't tell you anything. There's nothing to tell. Nothing that will help." He hiccuped. "Do they have booze in prison?"

For the briefest of moments, I could swear Amadeus Bozeman's face flashed a satisfied smile. "You don't have to talk to these women, Mr.

Fisher," Bozeman informed his client. "You have the right to remain silent, don't you?"

"Did you learn that in lawyer school, Dunk?" I dropped my voice to make it clear how little I thought of Amadeus Bozeman.

"Charming, Sasstra," Amadeus responded dryly with my old nickname from basic training. "I see we haven't matured all that much, have we?"

Fisher looked back and forth between us, his eyes glassy.

"Ignore them. Listen to me," Emma told him earnestly. "I really need your help. I need your help to do something only you can do. And it's going to help you. The prosecutor will make a deal with you for less time in prison if we find that painting unharmed. This gets worse for you if it's never recovered. A longer sentence. Think of your wife, your children. Don't you want to be there for them?"

Amadeus made a sound that seemed a lot like a snort.

Fisher stared back at Emma, trying to engage his brain within the pool of alcohol it undoubtedly swam in. "I know. I know I'm in bad. Bad things. I know. I was trying to make it better. You tell Gloria that, all right? I was trying to make it better. It'll be better for her this way."

"Trying to make what better?" Emma asked him.

"I'd advise you not to answer that," Amadeus Bozeman told his client in a steely voice. "Anything you say can be used against you, and you don't want the consequences to expand into anything the police don't already know about, do you?"

Will Fisher slunk lower in his chair, his eyes on his hands. He looked terrified.

"If you do that, you're lying, Mr. Fisher. You're lying to the police. You're lying by omission. You're not telling me everything, and by not telling me everything, you're making me think there's no chance you could possibly be innocent of any of these charges," Emma told him forcefully, her pointed finger slamming against the table in front of him. "If this is nothing more than you stealing? If there is no bigger story here? You're going to prison, Mr. Fisher, and I'm not gonna lose a minute's sleep over it."

"I am sorry, Detective," Fisher whispered. "I would tell you if I could. I'm a drunk, yeah. And I could've done better things with my life. But I'm not a bad man, you know." He stared at Emma with a sort of nervous defiance. "I have to do what I have to do." He glanced toward Amadeus. "I think...I think I'm done now."

"This interview's over," Bozeman told Emma. The two men stood up. "I think we'll take our chances in court. You don't have a painting. When you have it, and it has my client's fingerprints all over it, you give me a call. Now, if you'll excuse us, I need to meet with my client privately."

The attorney knocked on the door, and an officer led them both out.

"Get me into his cell," I told Emma. "That guy was still drunk. I bet you dollars to donuts he's been muttering, talking to himself."

She glanced at the door, then back at me. "Yeah, okay. Let's go."

I FOLLOWED her through the maze of hallways until we finally reached the cell block. The correction officer leading us seemed slightly annoyed we interrupted his early dinner. Still, he smiled brightly when Emma dismissed him after opening Will's cell. "We got it from here."

"What are you guys looking for?" the guard asked curiously.

"Astra talks to objects," she said, pointing. "Yesterday, we paid her to do that, but now she's doing it for free. She's going to tell me what the cell overheard."

The guard frowned. "Did you say what the cell overheard? Like, it's bugged?"

"No, more like the walls? They listen. Everything listens. You know how we think we're alone sometimes, and no one's watching and no one can hear us, so we let loose?" Emma asked him cheerfully. The guard nodded. "Yeah, that really isn't as private as we think it is."

The young officer looked at the walls as if he suddenly didn't trust them. Then he glanced up at the ceiling. "Um. Okay. So, when you guys need me to lock it back up again, let me know." He turned on his heel and walked back toward the guard station, his fingers pushing on the walls as he went.

"You're getting awfully free with the paranormal explanations," I told Emma.

"Everyone knew what you were doing working for the police department. How else am I supposed to explain why I took you in here?"

"Right, but I'm not an employee anymore. You

don't need to tell everyone what I'm doing or why," I said with a shake of my head, then nodded toward the cell. "What do you want me to find? Am I listening for anything important, or do you just want me to repeat everything?"

"Just repeat anything you hear," Emma answered, her eyes casting about the messy cell. "He's been in here less than a day. How did this place get so messed up?"

"He was pretty drunk in the interview. He had to be completely out of it when they arrested him. Wait," I turned and looked at her. "I thought you arrested him. How drunk was the guy?"

"I did arrest him, and I wouldn't have thought he was all that drunk. He could stand up. He could speak without slurring too much. He didn't sway on his feet. Come to think of it, Will Fisher looked—and smelled—more inebriated in that interview than he did when I grabbed him this morning." Emma looked around, scanning for a hiding spot. "There." She crossed the cell and moved rolls of toilet paper on a shelf to the side. "A bottle of vodka. And not just any vodka. Grey Goose. This stuff isn't cheap."

"Who could sneak a bottle that size into here?" I asked, but even as the words left my mouth, I realized there was only one person who could.

"Amadeus Bozeman. He could slip it right into his briefcase."

"Why would an attorney want his client drunk?" Emma asked, confused. "Wouldn't you want your client to sober up? Drunk clients run their mouths and tell the police things they never would've told them sober. I love interrogating drunk perps. They are way too easy." The detective held up the bottle. "So, here's my issue."

"What's your issue?"

"If Amadeus Bozeman did deliver this bottle to Will for sure, technically we're breaching attorney-client privilege by having you peek and eavesdrop on the bottle. On the other hand, I'm betting this bottle has a lot of tales to tell."

I walked forward and grabbed the bottle of Grey Goose from Emma's hand. "There is nothing in the law that says I have to respect attorney-client privilege. I'm not a cop, I'm not an attorney, I'm not a judge. I'm just that crazy psychic lady that lives with her mom." I walked out of the cell. "Come on."

"Where are you going? What about the cell?"

"Will Fisher is a drunk. This bottle was probably in his hand every moment he was in that cell, and it saw more than a stationary wall ever could." Emma followed me out of the cell and closed the door. "Let's go back to my place. I have some tools there that might help."

"Okay," the detective nodded.

I also had a sister that was a wizard at potions, I thought to myself.

Althea probably already had something whipped up to remove a vampire hypno-glamour right off an unsuspecting human. Getting Emma back to Arden House would give me a chance to peel off some of the control her brother had wrapped around her.

Hopefully, I could do it before the sun set.

CHAPTER EIGHT

$\mathcal{A}$mi met Emma and me at the front door as if she sensed us coming. With a cheerful greeting, Emma high-fived Ami and took off toward the kitchen in hopes, I suspected, that Aunt Gwennie was preparing something decent for dinner.

The sun's glow through the window reminded me I was running out of time. I was eager to get at least one step accomplished in Emma's release from her brother's control. So far, Rex had been winning. Time to turn the tide.

"Astra," Ami said, touching me on the shoulder. She had a slight smile on her face, her long skirt flowing behind her, gathering at her ankles. "What was that about? What's Emma acting so cheerful about?"

"In a minute." I scanned the house for any open windows or doors just to be safe. "Did we put the wards back up? The ones that keep vampires off the property?"

"Of course we did. You don't think Mom would leave those down, do you? Why?" She looked over her shoulder toward the kitchen. "Did you say something in front of Emma? Something that would make Rex angry?"

I said a lot of things that would provoke the vampire, and I had no doubt he'd show up here when it got dark. I mean, my entire day had been spent basically mumbling the equivalent of "come at me, bro."

I nodded and told her "Rex has used his vampire powers on his sister. I need Emma's head clear because I think he might be connected to this case." And because Rex sticking his hand in his sister's mind and twisting her up was so many levels of wrong, I could barely explain. "And to do that, I need Althea. Where is she?"

Ami thought about it, then pointed toward the stairs. "Still in her room, I think."

I nodded, turned, and hurried up the stairs.

Althea was stripping her bed when I found

her in her room, earbuds in her ears. "Althea," I said. She stuffed the stripped sheets into her pillowcases while hopping in time to the music, humming some song I didn't recognize. Her dark hair was pulled into a messy bun, the edges of her hair damp with sweat. "Althea!" I shouted, banging my hand on the door.

My fifteen-year-old sister jumped and turned, her eyes wide. Then, pulling the earbuds from her ears, she panted, "Holy jumping juniper tree, Astra! You scared the Hades out of me! I didn't even know you were home."

"Do you have a potion that breaks a vampire's hypnosis hold on a human?" I asked. "Rex has twisted Emma's head up something fierce, and I suspect he's done it against her will. Can we break that hold?"

"Oh," she says, wide-eyed, absorbing the news. "Oh, man." Althea took a deep breath, let it out, and stared at me intently. "So, wait. You *suspect* she didn't consent, or you *know* she didn't consent? I don't like giving people potions unless they know exactly what they are taking and what it will do. Can she understand what it's going to do?"

"If you're asking me whether she told me outright that she didn't consent? No, she didn't.

But considering she now believes reality is entirely different than it is, and she's sure it has always been that way, could I believe her if she told me?" I looked up at the ceiling and sighed. "Besides, who would want their mind toyed with like that?"

Althea raised her eyebrow. "Honestly, you'd be surprised," she said dryly, her voice tinged with amusement. "So...okay. I'll give it to her on principle. Vampire hypnosis is potent and can have some pretty nasty side effects. But I want to point out Emma may have volunteered to have her head sparkled. If she did, whacking her back into a reality she wanted to escape from? That might not be something she thanks you for."

"I get it," I told her. "I'll deal with it."

Althea nodded, grabbed her pillowcases of laundry, and headed toward the door. "I'll drop these off in the laundry room, grab the potion and find you guys."

"I think Emma's in the kitchen," I told her and turned to head back downstairs.

Althea's words, though, gnawed at me.

What if she wanted Rex to mess with her head? What if she wished to change the reality that so pained her?

No.

No one would voluntarily sign up to be effectively brainwashed. Least of all, Emma Sullivan. She valued her independence as much as anyone I'd ever met.

And had she consented to have Rex change her beliefs to fit what he wanted from her? This had to be the first stage of it, the first stage of what she consented to—but what else would he change? Make her hate me? Make her a corrupt cop? She couldn't agree to any of that now that her brain wasn't her own.

No.

I couldn't let Emma be manipulated like this.

MY ENTIRE FAMILY—AND Emma—gathered in the kitchen. Ayla watched quietly, occasionally nodding as if someone only she could hear was speaking to her.

"Well, that's just absolutely fascinating, Emma," my mother chirped. She walked imperiously toward the detective. "Emma, darling, you have something on your forehead here. Just let me get that smudge for you." My mother reached forward with her thumb.

At her touch, a sound like a paddle hitting a

ping-pong ball echoed in the kitchen. Emma's head immediately sank gently as her eyes closed. It was creepy, actually—like watching a skylight go dark.

Mom's smiled disappeared with the detective's conscious awareness, and she looked up at me. "Amadeus Bozeman was at your police department?"

"Can you teach me how to do that?" I asked her, ignoring her question.

"No," my mother answered sharply. "Amadeus Bozeman?"

What was the point of having "The High Priestess of Athena" as my mother if all I got out of the deal was an unpaid job as a bodyguard and owl clean-up duty? "I didn't know you knew who he was," I said.

She looked at me with annoyance. "Just because we didn't live in Imperatorial City, Astra, doesn't mean we didn't keep up with the politics of the witch world. So, of course, we know who he is."

"Very nasty man, that one," Aunt Gwennie added. "Solidly deficient in any sense of morality. Though, of course, that's who they trained him to be, the Council. So it's not surprising." My aunt glanced at me as if suddenly remembering I, too, was who the Council trained me to be. I raised my eyebrow. "It was different, dear. You were military."

"What is that horrible man doing in Forkbridge?" my mother demanded. "Emma said you spoke to him privately. Did he say what he wanted?"

I quickly explained everything that had happened during the day to my mother, my aunt, and my sisters. "Bozeman all but admitted to me that he's pulling some kind of scam. I don't know what it is, though. Theft? Embezzlement? Why pose as a human attorney? Why represent Will Fisher? Why does Will Fisher look nervous around his own attorney?"

"And what are the answers, then?" my mother asked.

I frowned, suddenly realizing just how many questions had no answers yet. "I don't know. But on top of all that, he claimed Rex invited him here to Forkbridge." I glanced at the snoring Emma. "Does that mean her brother is involved?"

"That's a lot of questions," Ami said.

"You're doing all this even though nobody's paying you?" Ayla asked, confused.

I shrugged. "Well, we still have to keep Will Fisher from being murdered."

Ayla frowned with a sour expression. "What's this *we* stuff, kemosabe? I'm just the store clerk, remember?" She shot a fierce glare at my mother.

"Ayla, dear, a linguistics professor has a theory about the origin of that word," my mother asked told Ayla. "Would you like to know the theory behind kemosabe?"

Ayla gave her another glare. "No."

Mom ignored that. "From the word *giimoozaabi*. It means 'one who sneaks.'" Ayla's cheeks turned pink, coloring her sullen expression. "Perhaps if you were more inclined to follow my instructions as opposed to sneaking around behind my back, you'd be more involved in the things that interest you." Mom sighed. "One of these days, Ayla Arden, you're going to invite something in that you won't be able to get rid of."

Ayla looked around, eyes hooded, shifting from side to side in uncomfortable silence. Finally, she huffed, "Fine. Never mind. I'll just listen."

Mom nodded once, a satisfied look on her face.

"While all this is fascinating, Emma already has that problem." I glanced out the window. "The sun is setting quickly. Suppose Rex can see and hear everything that she's saying and doing throughout the day while he is sleeping. In that case, he's going to make a beeline for this house the moment the sun dips below the horizon."

"Right." Althea took a deep breath. "So, Astra, all I can do is remove any effect on her mind from vamp hypnotism. It's not gonna do anything to the vampire bond between her and Rex. I don't think." She looked at me across the counter, her eyes sharp.

"I get it. We need his blood."

Althea nodded. "I just want to make sure that you understand the limitations of this potion." My sister placed a teacup on the counter and poured the hot water into it. She then pulled a vial from her pocket and held it up. "This is a one-trick pony. It does one thing. Now, it does that thing well, but it's not the potion to cut the tie between them."

I pointed at the cup. "Yep. I get it. Let's go. Heard you the first time."

Althea stuck her tongue out and poured the vial carefully into the cup.

"Another thing we need to be aware of," Aunt Gwennie added. "Although Rex didn't mention it, I don't believe the wards have any effect on the vampire blood bond whatsoever. That's how he tracked her here before. But that also means any time Emma is in this house, it's highly likely that Rex can hear every word we say. We'd always assumed when he was asleep, he wasn't aware of anything. Since Emma told you differently?" Aunt Gwennie clucked her tongue. "He knows more than we thought."

My mother nodded. "And, Astra, he'll know what you did."

"Good," I muttered. I looked toward the window. "I hope he does show up. Frankly, I have a whole lot of questions for him." The last rays of sunlight disappeared beneath the horizon. "Guys, we need to hurry up. It's dusk."

My mother chanted under her breath. Then she tapped Emma on the forehead again, and the detective's eyes popped open. "Have some tea, dear," my mother said, taking the cup from Althea and placing it in front of Emma. "We've been trying a new herbal blend. I'd love to get a human perspective on the taste."

"Oh, wow, I think I smell lilac," Emma said. She picked up the cup and looked inside it. "Pretty color. It almost looks sparkly." She drank the tea slowly, her eyes fixed on the swirling steam as it vanished in the air. "Oh, wow, that was—"

The cup, which had been balanced with one hand, fell from Emma's grasp splintered into shards as it hit the floor. Aunt Gwennie moved swiftly to clean up while the rest of us stared.

Emma's face, her expression, twisted with fury, her eyes wide, her teeth clenched. "He lied to me," Emma whispered. "No, wait, not...lie. He changed what I knew. Changed what I believed. My brother messed with my head!"

"I know. Take a deep breath, Emma," I told her. "Just breathe. Calm down."

"Calm down? Calm down?" The detective leaned forward in her chair and furrowed her brow. "Rex's voice was in my head but...but...it was as if it was my voice. Memories of things that never happened. They're fake, they never happened, but they're still there! I can see them!" Her chair flew back as she stood up and pounded her fist on the table. "In my own mind! How could he do that to me?"

"So, I'm guessing she didn't consent," Althea observed matter-of-factly.

Emma's face twisted, eyes bulged so far out they looked like they might burst free of their sockets. Her mouth moved, opening and closing as if they were trying to find words that just wouldn't come. Finally, the detective settled on five words, and those words seethed with furious anger. "I'm going to kill him."

"Well, technically, he's already dead," Ayla pointed out. "So, you know, really nothing for you to do there."

Ami leaned over and whispered, "Not the time for logic, sis."

I felt terrible for Emma.

I could see from her expression that she was devastated at the betrayal, and yet...I had this weird flash of instinct that her brother, maybe, wasn't a bad guy.

I blinked.

Where the heck was that coming from?

I sifted through what I knew of Rex in my mind. Yes, okay, he was mobbed up. Yes, he had invited Amadeus Bozeman to Forkbridge—maybe. Yes, he didn't want his sister anywhere around me. And yes, he had messed with her mind against her will.

And yet...

It was possible what Rex had done to Emma wasn't done out of hatred or malice or manipulation, but to protect her, to protect their relationship. That he was a vampire? It had to be a secret he was desperate to keep hidden here in Forkbridge.

Emma told me repeatedly how much her parents mourning Rex wounded her. I could see the temptation for a paranormal brother to not just fix that for her but hypnotize it away as if it never happened.

It didn't make it right, but people weren't perfect. He might have done all this because it was the only thing he knew to do to fix things for her.

Even if my nagging instinct of understanding was right?

None of this meant I wouldn't stake him if I had to.

MY EYES LOCKED on the tree line at the edge of the backyard. Now that Rex had settled down in Forkbridge, I was sure that was the direction he would come. It was the most private, with the least chance of being seen by townspeople.

Ayla stood outside with me. I could sense her anxiety.

"He won't hurt you," I told her quietly.

"He already hurt his sister," Ayla said. "If he could do what he did to Emma, why wouldn't he hurt me?" My younger sister glanced up at me. "I like ghosts a lot better than vampires. Ghosts can't hurt people."

"Vampires just don't mess with kids, and whether you accept it or not, you are still a kid. So I figure there must be a reason for it." The breeze kicked up, lashing Ayla and me with the wind. "Ugh, Florida. Come on. I really hope I don't have to have this conversation in the rain."

"The one with me or the one with Rex?"

Before I could answer, the patio door slid open, and Emma stepped out. "Any sign of my brother?" she asked.

"The ghosts say no one showed up yet," Ayla told her.

Emma frowned. "I thought vampires could move really fast?"

"They can," I said. The delay in his arrival— again—was making me question my assumptions. Could he be dealing with guilt? Trying to decide how to apologize to his sister? "It may take him a little longer, but I'm sure he'll be here."

"Maybe he can't face me unless he's controlling me," Emma said, her voice edged with anger. "It certainly seems like he prefers to deal with people by forcing them to see things his way." She turned and I noticed her face looked drawn. "You think my brother might be involved in whatever this conspiracy is with the insurance company, don't you?"

"I think your brother has information," I said simply. "I want to know what it is."

"Astra!" Ayla whispered. She pointed.

Out of the corner of my eye, I saw movement at the tree line near the woods. The branches shook as the wind suddenly picked up again, telegraphing an evening storm struggling to come to life. Finally, shifting shadows at the edge of the backyard morphed into a shape.

That shape took a few steps toward the property line and then stopped.

Rex.

"It's him," Ayla told us both.

I turned to my sister and pointed at the back door. "Go inside. Now." Just because vampires rarely hurt children didn't mean I was risking Ayla. She set her stubbornness aside and did what I told her to do without complaint or delay.

"He can't come up here, can he?" Emma asked me.

"Nope. We can go down whenever you're ready, or you can stay here and let me go talk to him. Realize, though, he can hear this entire conversation. His hearing is extremely sensitive. Wards can't block that out. That, and your blood bond is still active. So anything you say, he'll hear."

Staring across the yard, Emma's hands clenched. "Not like that's any different from any other day," she finally answered.

Rex stepped slightly closer to the edge of the backyard with his hands in his pockets. He said nothing, didn't gesture. He just stood there watching us. His expression was hard to read from this distance.

"You have no idea how much I want to punch you in the face," I breathed.

His head tilted at my words.

"I can't see him right now. I'm just too angry," Emma admitted finally.

I nodded. "I get it. You do whatever you need to do for yourself. I can handle it."

"I know you can. I should go inside, then."

"That's a good idea."

But she didn't.

It seemed a year went by while we stood in silence, waiting for Emma to turn away from Rex. I didn't want to leave her here alone to go talk to the vampire, and, to be honest, I wanted her inside with the others. Her emotions were running high, and I knew my family could stop her from doing something impulsive if her fury got the best of her.

Finally, she whispered, "You violated my trust. You've warned me over and over again that Astra would betray me. That her family would betray me. But you took me away from myself, Rex." Emma choked up, took a breath, and continued. "You put fake memories in my mind. The Ardens gave me complete control of myself back. They trust me to be able to handle all this paranormal stuff. You don't. What's more, you used it on me. You manipulated me. At some point, I'll talk to you, and I'll be expecting one hell of an apology."

Rex's head dropped, and his shoulders slumped.

"But for right now, I can't see you. I love you. You're my brother. You're my only brother. I loved you as a human. I love you as a vampire. Just because I love you, though, doesn't mean I'm gonna let you play with my head like it's your personal Barbie Dream House." She stepped forward. "You want to earn my trust back? Tell Astra what she wants to know. That's a start."

Rex nodded. Emma nodded back. Then she turned her back on her brother and went inside the house. A second later, the patio door slid open, and Emma stuck her head out. "Don't stake him," she warned me. "I mean it, Astra."

Reluctantly, I agreed.

She closed the door and went inside again.

"Just you and me now," I breathed.

Rex nodded.

"Not even close, smarty pants!" Archie shouted from somewhere in the trees. "Like you're ever alone. Please! I'm the goddess's own owl! I know my—" The branches rustled violently. "Sorry, got distracted. Squirrel."

I smiled and stepped off the porch to confront Emma's brother.

CHAPTER NINE

"You know, if you just shove your fist over the boundary line really fast," Archie called from the branches above my head, "the most you would lose is a finger, and that's only if he's fast. You could smash his pale, patrician vampire nose from there with a fast jab. I bet Emma would send you a thank you card."

Rex Sullivan looked like he'd had a fitful night —um, day—and too many thoughts to sleep soundly. I didn't know what vampires did during the day, not really. Was the sleep restorative as it was for humans and witches? Or were they—as rumored—effectively dead? "Archie, rein it in for a second, will you?"

"Fine. I'll be quiet. But I'm not leaving," the owl grumbled ominously.

Rex gave me a small, condescending smile. "I suppose you think you've won now. With one potion, you broke the psychic bond I had with my sister."

"She's still your sister. That's a bond. And frankly, I didn't think this was some kind of competition, Rex. You turned it into that." I studied Rex with a practiced eye. He stood casually and seemed relaxed. No tension in his body to indicate an imminent threat. "When I met you, I thought you and I would be friends. I don't know what changed from—"

"Don't play stupid," he said coldly, the sarcastic smile fading. "You know exactly what changed."

I blinked in surprise at the icy tone of his voice.

Which, if you think about it?

It was silly.

Obviously, Rex would be furious with me for wrecking the bamboozlement of his sister. My family's ability to break his hold over Emma put a damper on whatever his plans were. So, of course, he'd be angry at me.

But there was...something else there.

Something I couldn't put my finger on.

As I stared, Rex shifted as if he were suddenly nervous. I couldn't figure out if he was jumpy or it was a ploy to make me see him as weak, to make me drop my guard.

"No, dude, I don't know what changed," I told him. "I just assumed when you and I worked on the pixie case, you were entirely disingenuous. You know, pretending to be a polite, normal dude for…I don't know, reasons?" I held up my hands. "But this isn't really about me, is it?"

"What I did to Emma was entirely about you," Rex shot back. "I was handling the situation with her—and my family—until you showed up." The invisible border stood between us, the only thing keeping the two of us on our sides. "Without warning, you show up from Paranormopolis and bring all that drama to this little Florida town."

I frowned, puzzled. "What drama? What are you even talking about?" I glared across the boundary, waiting for a response, but Rex just looked away. "Forkbridge doesn't have any Paranormopolis drama. I got fired, I got on the train, and I came home. That's it."

Rex turned back, met my eyes, but said nothing.

"You know, I came home to the town I grew

up in? You and I may be the most dramatic thing going on in Forkbridge right now unless you count the car show at Griselda's." I squinted suspiciously. "Well, until you brought Amadeus Bozeman here."

"You really are unbelievable, Astra, you know that? You act like I'm the only one that's ever done anything villainous," Rex told me with scorn he clearly felt deeply. "You fugitive trackers in your arrogance and your perfect fascist-level surety of purpose—"

I bristled at that level of venom. "Hey, mafioso? You want to rein in the seething contempt a little bit?" I crossed my arms. "I'll admit there are things that I did that I am not proud of. But, someone gave me an order, an assignment, and off I went like a good little soldier. In retrospect, I didn't earn a whole bunch of karma points for the things I did. I get that. I live with that." I leaned forward. "But unlike you, I thought I was doing the right thing. And unlike you, I never killed anyone."

"Oh, really?" He sounded like I'd just kicked his dog. "What about Valeria Scott?"

"Who the heck is Valeria Scott?" I asked him. "I don't know anyone by that name. Should I?"

"You would if you remembered the names of

those you kill. I, at least, managed that much respect for the dead. But I guess you don't even give them that courtesy, do you?" We stared at each other solemnly. "All of you that worked for the Witches' Council—we were always nothing to you."

"I didn't work for the Witches' Council. I worked for the government. I was part of the military. Did my work dovetail into some pretty shady stuff the Witches' Council pulled? Sure. Absolutely. I'm not gonna deny that, even if I didn't let myself realize it at the time. But you knew that. You knew what I did for a living when I met Emma, and you sang my praises. And you know my military work stopped as soon as I moved to Forkbridge—"

"Then why is Valeria Scott dead?" Rex asked me. "You staked her just a month ago when—"

I blinked. "Whoa, wait a minute. Back up, there, you oversized mosquito. I didn't stake anybody a month ago."

Rex rolled his eyes.

"Don't do that."

"Do what?" Rex said, sounding a little exasperated.

"The condescending eye roll. I have three younger sisters and an owl familiar. I can promise you that won't work on me. You're just wasting my time."

"I'm simply expressing an opinion without speaking," Rex told me coldly. "If you want me to say it, I'll say it. You're lying. You must be lying because Val is dead, and you are here. It's not proof of guilt, but it's certainly suspicious."

Those two facts didn't seem related at all. How they got tied up into a knot in the vampire's mind, I didn't know. Maybe I should just follow Archie's advice to punch the vampire square in the face. It seemed as good an option as any.

The light from the house cast shadows across his face, outlining his chin. Rex's expression was grave. It was concerned, pained, as if a kaleidoscope of negative emotions were fighting for prominence. Vampires were notoriously expressionless and hard to read. That I could see anything in his face at all was unusual.

I stared.

He stared back.

I'd wrestled for the past few hours with a nagging suspicion something was going on with Rex. Something beyond the vampire just being a psychotic criminal who felt it was easier to manipulate Emma than to talk to her. Something more than just his hatred of me and his misogynistic need to control his sister.

Nothing Rex said changed my knee-jerk assumption...but the feeling there was more to him still nagged at me.

Yes, he'd had a level of power and control over his sister with that vampire blood bond I couldn't fathom. And yes, he used it to bend Emma to his will. But knowing some crimes vampires have been accused of? Rex Sullivan could have done far worse, with far more impact, with far less subtlety.

I took a steadying breath.

"Look, Rex, I have no reason to put in the effort it would take to lie to you. None. And as much as I've had the urge to shove a chopstick through your chest multiple times over the past month, I haven't."

"Yet."

"Dude, I've never staked a vampire in my entire life!" Rex, his mouth flattened in anger, give a quick exhale of breath to ensure I knew he didn't believe me. I ignored it. "For one, blood is tough to get out of this uniform, and you people die messily. And two—and this is the most important point—I'm not a murderer."

"Well, that's not what Amadeus Bozeman

says." The words startled me like an unexpected punch. "He told me you killed Valeria."

AND THERE IT WAS.

I'd known something was beneath the surface. How I'd known, though, I couldn't have told you. Maybe I had some residual insight into Rex since I'd touched him before. Maybe Ami's gift was rubbing off on me. Perhaps I'd just gotten good at reading people over the years.

"Amadeus Bozeman is a liar. Again, I don't kill people," I responded immediately, firmly, and without hesitation. "Let's back up. You still haven't answered my question. Who is Valeria Scott, and why do you even care that she's dead?"

"Val was everything to me," Rex whispered, his head dropping as if the weight of his memories were pulling it down. "She was hundreds of years old. She'd learned so much in the dozens of lifetimes she lived."

"I see." Valeria Scott, if hundreds of years old, was an elite vampire that had mastered survival. Most vampires didn't make it past one hundred years, and their violent second-act lives often ended in tragedy. Older vampires were practically worshiped in the vampire world for the knowledge they carried, the history they'd seen, and the secrets they presumably knew. "When was she turned?"

"The sixteen hundreds, I think." Rex waved his hand in the cool night air. "It's not about who she was, though. It's about what Val did for me. She helped me get away from the Salvatores. Showed me how to live in the shadows. To thrive in the human world without killing. While doing good at times, believe it or not." Rex's head snapped up as if he just remembered who he was talking to. His eyes fired with anger. "Until you killed her."

He truly believed I killed his friend. I could see it.

Just as obviously, Amadeus Bozeman lied about who murdered her and specifically lied that I'd been the one to end her long immortal life. The fake lawyer must have done that for a reason —and it was mighty suspicious he did it right before winding up in Emma's theft investigation. The same research I got thrown into thanks to Athena's durn sparkle card.

Too many coincidences.

But where's the pivot?

Where was the dangling thread to pull so it would all unravel?

I still couldn't see it.

The death of Rex's friend at "my" hand, though, was a good motivation to want me away from his sister. Had it been true—if one of my sisters had hypothetically become close to Emma's hypothetical murderer—I might have acted the same way as Rex. Break ethics, bend morality. It was somewhat understandable.

That's not even considering the fact that killing a vampire several hundred years old was no small feat. Anyone that would do so was not just fearless.

They were ruthless.

"Did you reach out to Amadeus Bozeman about Valeria, or did he reach out to you?" I asked, my voice softening.

"He reached out to me just over a month ago to let me know she was dead. The agency that handled her affairs in the human world is, oddly enough, in Forkbridge." Why would a several-hundred-year-old vampire have her financial affairs centered in Forkbridge of all places? "Amadeus said he knew Val and I were close, and she wanted me to know what happened to her."

That made me blink.

How did Bozeman know Val and Rex were close?

Vampires didn't exactly broadcast their personal business to the paranormal world. They were notoriously secretive creatures. "Did you know Amadeus Bozeman before he contacted you? Did she?" I asked.

His eyes narrowed. "I'd heard of him. Everyone's heard of him. But no, we were not acquainted in any way. I don't know that Val knew him, but it wouldn't surprise me, considering her age. She knows—she knew— many people," Rex said, his voice heavy with emotion. "Why are you asking me these questions?"

"Because I didn't kill Valeria Scott."

"So you said." Rex smiled. And it wasn't a strange, comedy relief smile, either. It was an I'd-kill-you-if-I-could smile. "I don't believe you. Why should I believe you?"

Instead of lashing out at him again for the mind-manipulating stunt he pulled with his kid sister, I decided to trust him. A little.

Even if he didn't trust me.

"Because Amadeus Bozeman, who claimed I killed your friend, showed up at the police station today, in the center of your sister's insurance theft case, as an attorney. Because a goddess wants me to protect an agent from that same insurance agency, and that agent I'm charged with protecting? He's represented by Amadeus Bozeman."

Rex froze motionless, taking a long moment to consider my words. Finally, the vampire blinked. "Those are—"

I cut him off. "If that's not enough to make you wonder, all these things are happening while you, Emma, and I are running around being suspicious of each other, fighting with each other, and being at loggerheads with each other." I tilted my head. "That's a spaghetti-mess of coincidences, don't you think?"

"I don't believe in coincidences," Rex said quietly.

"Me, neither."

He tilted his head. "I still don't trust you."

"Clearly. You got me fired from my job."

Rex studied me as if trying to decide whether his assumptions about me might be wrong after all. "About that," Rex said, raising his voice slightly. "Bozeman wanted you fired from the police department. He knew how I felt about you being close to Emma in light of what you did to Val, and he suggested I submit the complaint. He assured me it was the quickest way to get you away from her."

"Did he now?" I asked, though admittedly, I wasn't asking.

"He did."

Part of me still wanted to punch Rex right in the face.

Sure, okay, Amadeus said I murdered Rex's dusty, medieval vampire love, and that would spin anyone up. I got Rex's aggressive response. Maybe even grudgingly respected his coming at me a little. Even so…

Rex didn't come at me directly in response, though.

He used the blood bond to mess with Emma's head.

I couldn't get past that.

"Why manipulate your sister, though? Was that Bozeman's idea, too?" I asked Rex. "You had to know that if she ever realized what you'd done, she'd be furious."

Rex turned his head toward me and bobbed it quickly in affirmation.

"Then why?"

"I had the power to save her pain, so I used it."

I scoffed. "You didn't just use it. You used it maliciously."

"I didn't," Rex said, crossing his arms. "But you're right; I should have thought of a more clever approach to address her issues with me and to get her away from you." His face sort of cracked, a vulnerable expression shooting into his eyes for the briefest moment. "She didn't deserve the pain I inflicted."

I frowned. "No, she didn't, but you—"

"I'll talk about this with Emma, but you and I discussing it won't solve anything. I know how you feel and how she feels." He shoved his hand out like a crossing guard. "Maybe you didn't murder Val. But even so, I don't trust you. I don't like you. I don't doubt that you'd do something to my sister if doing so furthered your goals."

Shockingly, his view of me was much like the one I had of him.

Could we both be wrong?

Rex pointed at me. "Yes, I used a little of the bond to take away the worry over her job. Or, I should say, I used a lot of the bond to take away all her worry, to make her think everything was fine. It was a gamble, but she deserved that." He stood taller. "She and I will deal with the fallout between us. I will not discuss this further with you. I've violated her trust enough."

Rex's big brother-style affection for Emma was endearing. It made me like him a little, even though I was still a little suspicious.

I HAD JUST FINISHED TELLING Emma about the conversation between Rex and me. After minutes of silence, she finally spoke.

"Valeria Scott was his girlfriend or something?" Emma asked, frowning.

"Possibly. I didn't dig too deep. Once he told me the thing about Amadeus, I realized this is all tied up together. Rex, the case. Maybe even Valeria. I wanted to come and let you know about all of it." I frowned. "I think we need Rex involved. We need more information, and only he has it."

Emma nodded and admitted she didn't know an enormous amount about Rex's time as a vampire. "He told me about general stuff like politics and paranormals, but he never said much of anything about relationships he had." Rex's account left my friend with a deep crease of concern between her brows. "So, let me ask you point-blank. Did you believe him?"

I nodded. "I did, though I couldn't tell you why and…well, I'm not sure my instinct can be relied upon. I was predisposed to trust Rex when I met him because he was your brother, Emma." I shrugged. "Intellectually, I think he might be a lying snake. But my gut tells me that he's not. So I feel like what he said was true, but I'm also a little nervous about trusting that."

"I can do a reading on him," Ami offered.

"Could you?" Emma nodded. "Honestly, I want to stay angry at him. He deserves it. What he did?" She glowered toward the backyard, where Rex waited at the edge of the property. "But Astra's right. It sounds like he's in the middle of this whole mess, too."

Ami pulled out the ever-present tarot cards from her pocket and shuffled quickly. Sitting down next to Emma, she flipped over the first card—

—and the three of us stared, mouths wide.

Prickles of energy climbed up my spine as the unexpected plot twist glittered at me from the table. "The Star card," I deadpanned. "Now I have two people the goddess wants me to keep alive."

Ami raised her eyebrow. "And one's already dead."

CHAPTER TEN

*W*ell played, Fate.
Well played.

Ami dropped the cards and took off to get my mother, I ran out and through the backyard to heave Rex across the boundary, and Emma sank down on a lounge chair trying to process the evening's turn.

Initially, we'd chuckled at the absurdity of it.

Within a few moments, her laughter quickly turned to barely blinked-back tears.

Whatever Rex had done, whatever choices he had made?

Emma still loved him.

"Let's go," I told the vampire sharply, reaching

out with my open hand to grab his arm. He lifted his hand toward his body and stepped back. "Dude, come on. Let's go. You have to come inside."

"Where's Emma?" he asked.

"Inside." I reached out again. "Let's go."

"No." Rex crossed his arms. "I told you, I don't trust you."

My hand clenched into a fist, and then I dropped it. "You're going to have to get over that pretty quick. You need to come with me," I told him. "We've gotten notice that your life is in danger—"

"You can't be serious," Archie burst out from the branches above. "This nimrod deserves Athena's protection?" I gave a quick nod, sure that the owl could see me from wherever he was. "So now we have to protect two people? One moron in jail and the other an idiot vampire everybody's mad at?"

Rex glanced up. "You know, for a divine being, you certainly have your opinions."

"Really, brainiac? Does that surprise you? Have you read a single holy book from any religion anywhere in the world in your entire life or post-life?" the owl asked Rex with disbelief. "Divinity isn't exactly known for its lack of opinions about people. Sure, we do all that forgiveness stuff, but not before whacking you in the head a few times. We're carrot and stick kind of people, even with the omens and stuff."

"Vampires don't have gods," Rex responded simply. "And I certainly don't require anyone's protection or anyone's forgiveness."

My body went rigid with anger. "Oh, really? Not even Emma's?"

Rex frowned. "You know I didn't mean her."

"Look, I don't like this any more than you do, but Ami was doing a reading on you for Emma, and the Star card came up. That means your life is in danger, and the goddess Athena thinks you might be useful to somebody at some point in the future. So I have to keep you from dying." I pointed toward the house. "The best place for me to do that is in that house, so come on."

Rex stared at my hand suspiciously. "Do you have to touch me to do that?"

Oh, this guy was getting on my last nerve. "Yes, idiot. The reason you can't cross the boundary is that you're not welcome here. Since our unwelcoming stance has unexpectedly changed? For you to be welcome here, I have to grab you and pull you across."

"That works even with your gloved hand?"

"Yes." I held out my hand again. "Any day now, buddy."

Archie left his perch and flew between the trees silently. Without a sound from his mouth or wings, the owl circled over Rex once, then twice —and then rather unexpectedly landed on top of his head.

Rex stared at me, the bird balanced on his skull. "Is this," he pointed up, "really necessary?"

Archie tilted his head at a ninety-degree angle, staring down. "You're the one that didn't want to grab her hand. She has to protect you. I'm here to assist her. So, you know, until you cross the threshold and go into the house?" Archie picked his talons up and stepped from side to side as if he was settling in. "I have to be right in the center of the action to protect you." He shook his wing feathers. "This seems the best vantage point to stop an arrow. Or something." The bird lifted his head and winked once at me.

I stifled a laugh.

With a sigh of resignation, Rex reached out and took my hand. It was only—I suspected— because he was less than thirty seconds away from being pecked like a drum by the owl. Then, with a yank, he stumbled across the boundary.

The bird stayed balanced precariously on his head.

"Thank you. Can he go now?" Rex asked, pointing up at the owl. "I'm sure your wards can stop the arrow the bird was looking for."

"Archie is his own owl. He's not a trained pet I give commands to," I said. "Ask him to get off your head, and maybe he will now that you've done what he wants."

"Get off my head," he told the owl.

The bird turned his head and gave a quick puff of his chest feathers. Then with the last squeeze of Rex's head—a squeeze that made the vampire wince—Archie launched himself into the air and took flight.

"Do you think we should let Emma and fang boy go into another room and work out their differences? Or let her punch him before we get started?" Archie turned to Emma. "What do you think, doll-face? Do you want to take a few whacks at him?"

"Archie, you shouldn't encourage violence," Ami told him with a frown.

"That goddess you worship? Little-known fact. She's the goddess of two by fours to the head when people are stupid." Archie thrust his head out and stared at Rex with large eyes. "And if ignorance is bliss, you must be the happiest person on the planet right now."

"I'm standing right here, and I can hear you," Rex muttered with a glare at the bird. "You may have forgotten that."

"Why would I bother to insult you if you couldn't hear me?" The owl jumped to the center of the kitchen table, and my mother winced as his sharp talons scratched the wood. "I know you can hear me, fang-face."

"Am I the only one here that can't hear the owl?" Emma asked, looking around at my sisters, my mother, my aunt, and her brother. "You can all hear him and understand what he's saying?" We all murmured affirmatively. "Jeesh. Talk about being the odd one out." The detective glanced across the table at her brother and then dropped her eyes.

"Now that we are all here." Mom smiled and took her place at the head of the table. "According to Ami, the goddess has decided Astra must protect two beings and not just one," my mother announced (as if we all weren't aware of that already). "While this is unexpected, I'm sure it's because our family has done such an incredible job assisting Astra with her divine mission."

"Sure," I responded with a shrug. "It couldn't possibly be because I'm totally capable of keeping two people alive."

My mother's proud face fell.

"Astra, your mother is not saying anything about your capability." My aunt gave me a stern look, her eyes containing several warnings she didn't need to verbalize. "Emma's case looked quite simple in the beginning. A stolen painting, nothing more. But now?" She clicked her tongue. "Amadeus Bozeman in Forkbridge would've been cause for concern even if the Star card hadn't flipped over."

"Twice," Ami added as if we'd forgotten.

My mother nodded in agreement. "His presence here concerns us all." Mom leaned forward in her chair and nodded toward the vampire.

"Bozeman contacted me about a month and a half ago," Rex said quietly, his eyes fixed on me. "He told me that a woman I've known quite well over the last year had been killed by Astra. He also related that Val—the woman killed—wanted me to have her possessions, but her money was held in Paranormopolis. This, as you know, makes those assets difficult to use in the human world. Bozeman said she had an agency in Forkbridge that could process the money."

Emma gaped at her brother. "Process? You mean launder. They have to launder the money."

I looked at Emma. "The insurance agency. Could it be nothing more than a money-laundering operation?" That would explain the weird vibe I got from the place. It wasn't an insurance agency, not really.

"Anything can be a money-laundering operation," the detective responded. "You just have to have a source of illicit funds, a way to process it through, and someone at the other end that's going to use it for legitimate purposes."

"I don't think I'm following. What do you mean, launder money?" Ami asked.

"I saw this on *Law and Order* once!" Althea told her sister with excitement. "There are three stages to money laundering. The placement stage, the layering stage, and the integration stage. The placement stage is when illegitimate money is paid into legitimate financial accounts. The layering stage when the money is disguised by being moved in numerous transactions." Althea's eyes shined as she held forth on the intricacies of money laundering. "The integration stage is when the clean money is put back into circulation to fund other activities."

"Like a dance club?" I raised my eyebrow and glanced at Rex.

Althea nodded. "Anything legitimate. You just have to get it into a position where there's a legitimate reason for it."

"I need to start watching that show," Ayla said, her eyes wide. "You learned all that from TV?"

"If she did, my compliments. Your sister nailed it," Emma said.

"I still don't understand how you could do something like this with an insurance company," Aunt Gwennie said. "Insurance regulation is pretty strict, isn't it?"

"Criminals use insurance companies for money laundering by buying insurance," Emma told her. "Then they submit claims on the policy to retrieve their funds. Insurance policies can be structured as investments, too, like variable annuities and some life insurance policies. Anyway, they overfund their policies and move money in and out of different ones. Eventually, it's clean."

Althea nodded. "That way, they can establish a stream of innocent wire transfers or checks for a low cost. Just early withdrawal penalties."

"So we think the stolen painting claim is—possibly—a fraudulent claim just to get money out?" I asked.

"I have a question. Are you even sure there is a painting?" Althea asked me. "Just because someone has an insurance policy on a painting doesn't really mean the painting exists. Right, Emma? Especially if this place is crooked."

Emma and I looked at one another. "That would explain why an expensive painting was supposedly being housed in some cheap storage unit without environmental controls," the detective puzzled out. "It didn't matter where the painting was stored because there really was no painting."

I nodded. "Okay, suppose this is all true. I haven't heard anything explain what Amadeus Bozeman is doing in Forkbridge. What does he have to do with any of this?"

We all turned and looked at Rex.

Rex came out with the same answer he'd been

giving us all along. "I've told you as much as I know."

This time, Emma wasn't extending any benefits of the doubt.

"That hardly seems likely," Emma told him. "You took psychic and emotional control of a Forkbridge police detective. One assigned to deal with a case that you seem to be rather suspiciously right in the middle of." She crossed her arms. "And you suddenly have a whole lot of money to buy property, open a club, do construction—"

The vampire, in a mild and caring tone, leaned toward his sister. "Sweetie, I'm your brother—"

"Man, that *sweetie, baby* crap really doesn't work on me when your psychic grip's been pried off my head. I'm not a child, Rex. You know, if you were human and messed with my mind against my will, you'd be in jail. Brother or not." Emma's voice was harsh and angry. "How can I trust you? I'm not even sure I know you anymore."

Rex's face looked pained. "You know me. You know me better than anyone."

"Do I?" Emma paused, staring at the brother I knew she loved. Within seconds, her detective instincts took back over. "And by the way, if you knew so much—why didn't you pick up on the fact that I was working a case that had to do with you? Weren't you watching me all day?" Her eyes narrowed. "Your money came from the same insurance agency, didn't it? It had to. I mean, if we're right and they launder money. And what's more—"

I put a hand on Emma's arm. "So, not to derail this—because I really do enjoy watching you verbally slap your brother around—let's let him answer. Are we right?" I asked Rex.

"Until today, all I observed was a detective working on a case of a stolen painting. Yes, my money came through the same insurance agency," Rex admitted. "But there are many agencies that cycle paranormal money back into the human world. So I had no reason to be suspicious of anything. And other than your Star card, Astra, I don't have any reason to be suspicious of anything now."

"Wait a minute. Your friend was murdered, and you had no reason to be suspicious of anything?" I challenged him, my voice rising. "Did your brain synapses stop firing when your heart stopped or were you naturally this dense when you were alive, too?"

"I had no reason for suspicion. I was told you

were the one that killed her," he said with barely veiled bitterness. "And, frankly, I have nothing but your word that you didn't."

"I didn't."

"Liar," he growled.

"*Pax Templi*, children," my mother reprimanded both of us, but she was staring at Rex. "You've been given shelter here. You've been welcomed into our home and our covenstead and the goddess's temple." My mother brought herself straight and tensed, her voice hardening. "Do not growl at my daughter."

Rex dropped his head and muttered, "Apologies, priestess. It has been a difficult day." His expression barely concealed his contempt for me.

I glanced over at Emma.

Her angry expression made it clear she didn't trust her brother.

Well. This was going great.

I sighed. "Look. We have to find a way to trust each other, or we're never gonna get anywhere. With two Star cards, the goddess Athena's attention, Amadeus Bozeman in Forkbridge? I just think we have to find a way to trust one another."

"That's unlikely," Emma snorted. "Rex doesn't trust you, I don't trust him—"

"Ami doesn't trust me with the rabbits," Archie added with enthusiasm.

Ami glared.

"What do you suggest, Astra, dear?" Aunt Gwennie asked me.

I sighed again and removed my gloves.

To hide your true intentions and any traces of your misdeeds, you have to deceive through body language, attitude, demeanor. All at once, all working together. The more confident you are in your lie, the better the deception. Humans can, if they choose, become practiced and proficient liars.

What humans have to work to master, though, vampires can do by instinct. They are born to their second life as instinctive creatures of artful cunning, guile so inherent that disingenuousness is nearly perfect.

I couldn't be sure of anything with Rex unless I read him. I hoped Emma trusted me enough to rely on whatever I would find. Maybe then we could push through this telenovela-level of drama and actually, you know, catch the bad guy.

"What object are you reading?" Rex asked politely.

"You," I told him.

"That's not going to happen." Rex's face flushed pink, and I could see his anger flare at the mere suggestion. "I realize that I'm not the most popular person around this table; I understand what I did with Emma has caused a problem. But there are limits to what I'm willing to do to make up for my trespass." His eyes flashed with anger. "I am a vampire, and it's not in my nature or my temperament to render myself defenseless."

"What do you mean by defenseless?" Ami asked.

"Astra's military uniform has certain magical defenses woven into the very fabric. She was a fugitive tracker, and so those defenses were needed to apprehend magical creatures that did not wish to fall into the hands of the Witches' Council," he told Ami. "Although those defenses are no longer needed, she wears the outfit. That outfit ensures that her mind and what she thinks and what she intends are unreadable."

"What's wrong with that?" Ami asked.

"The vampire is being asked to willingly place

himself in her power even though her intentions are unknown," Aunt Gwennie offered. "His greatest defense is the ability to react in a split-second, to see what's coming the moment that it comes. It's more than just uncomfortable for Rex. He's like a turtle on his back while Astra pokes around his belly. It goes against his very nature as a vampire."

"So?" I asked. "A little discomfort never killed anyone."

Yeah, okay, maybe I was a little harsh.

And uncaring.

And unsympathetic.

Sue me.

"This is a temple of Athena, Astra," my mother reminded me. "We are required to respect the nature and beliefs of others." She gave me a speculative look. "While I know you don't follow our path, dear, you were brought up to respect the temple rules." My mother looked at me pointedly.

"Oh, fine," I mumbled and unzipped the front of my uniform to strip it off. "He's a vampire, and half of them are complete psychopaths, but sure, I wouldn't want to offend his sensibilities."

"Astra!" my mother called out sharply.

I stopped unzipping and looked up at her.

"Are you using the mom voice because of my snarky commentary or because I'm about to get naked in the middle of the living room? I'm not sure which thing you want me to stop."

Now her face reddened with anger.

Very un-priestess-like.

"I have some clothes you can put on, Astra. They should be dry." Althea grabbed me and dragged me toward the laundry room. Once there, she pulled out a pair of sweatpants and a t-shirt. "That should fit decently enough for what you need to do."

I nodded, closed the laundry room door, and pulled my uniform off. Then, with a deft balance, I slipped into the casual outfit Althea let me borrow.

"Oh, wow," my sister breathed.

"What? Is some body part sticking out somewhere?" I looked down and tugged the shirt this way and that, looking for a hole. "Is Mom going to lose it because I'm not wearing a bra? What?"

"No, it's just that I haven't seen you in street clothes since you left for the military, and I only know that from pictures since I was so young. I think this is the first time in my entire life I've laid eyes on you out of uniform that I can remember," Althea said, her eyes watering. "I don't even know why it's affecting me so much. I'm not very emotional. Normally." She looked up into my eyes. "Astra, you're really pretty. You look so soft in regular clothes. Like a school teacher."

"Well, Thea, now you understand why I don't wear regular clothes," I told her. Her emotional reaction to my quick change made me slightly uncomfortable, and I hurried out of the laundry room.

I hustled in and pointed to the vampire. "Okay, let's get on with this—"

Rex's face was white.

"Oh, dear goddess, what's wrong now?" I asked.

"I'm so sorry," he whispered, his expression mortified. "I had no idea your feelings for Emma ran so deep, or your loyalty was so unshakable. I sincerely, truly apologize for the problems that I've caused between the two of you—"

"That's nice," I said dismissively, pulling up a chair next to him. "Let's get this over with. Come on, give me your hand."

Concentrating, his guarded eyes searching my face, Rex said with surprise, "You didn't kill Val."

"I believe I told you that, but in case you need to hear it again? No, I didn't kill Val. Never met

Val. I don't know Val. Never killed a vampire. We good?" I reached out to grab Rex's hand, but he pushed his chair back out of my reach. He looked...fearful. "Hey, Rex? I actually need to hold on to you to use my little psychic power. I know yours works by proximity, but I'm not that lucky."

"You sure you have control of the energy?" he asked me.

"Would you stop screwing around and just give me your hand?"

"Wait a minute. What energy, Rex?" my mother asked.

"The goddess energy coursing through her entire body." The vampire looked up, confused, at the baffled faces of the witches around him. "Can none of you sense it? Once Astra removed her uniform, the room practically filled with it. It's like standing next to an electrical transformer."

"Huh. That's interesting. That's very interesting," Archie muttered.

I eyed the raptor. "What's so interesting?"

"Well, you got the energy the first night I showed up. I mean, I gave it to you. But you hadn't done all that much with it, so I figured it just wasn't gonna manifest outwardly in you. You're pretty capable all on your own, so I just figured maybe it didn't have to." The owl marched toward the edge of the table and looked up into my eyes. "Everybody metabolizes a big old glob of goddess energy differently, you know? So anyway, it never occurred to me your suit was tamping down on it."

"Right. That. The sparks a few days ago. Got it." I looked at Rex. "Can we get on with this, please?"

Nope.

My family wasn't done discussing Rex's observation.

"I don't sense anything," Aunt Gwennie said. "Girls?" My sisters all shook their heads no. "Minnie, what do you think? Why could this vampire sense this *goddess energy* when we can't?"

"Can't we talk about this later?" I asked in frustration. "We have a case. Two cases, actually. I don't know if you guys remember, but there's usually a clock running on people?"

My mother looked at me thoughtfully, ignoring my words. "I don't know, Gwen. It may have something to do with the fact that we are priestesses. We are trained to sense the goddess's energy everywhere. A little bit more or a little bit less wouldn't be all that noticeable to us." Mom glanced at the vampire. "What do you sense,

Rex? Exactly? If you had to describe it in one word."

He eyed me warily. "Danger."

"Maybe that's why we don't sense it," Ayla chimed in. "It's no threat to us." Ayla looked at Archie. "Do you know how she should try and use it?"

"It's always better to ask before shooting the place up with lasers." The bird turned toward me and placed his wings in the area of what should be hips. "So, I may be wrong about this, but here's my theory. You were given goddess energy from a star goddess, right? Athena makes a Star card come up. So, make a star in your palm and wish on it."

"Make a star in my palm and wish on it," I repeated slowly. Archie nodded. "And how, pray tell, does one *make* a star?"

"A star is born when atoms of light are squeezed. The nuclei have to undergo fusion," Althea explained. "The force of gravity compresses the atoms until the fusion reaction starts."

"In other words, make a fist," Archie told me, "and concentrate."

Concentrating, I imagined gathering light and making it dense on the center of my palm. I closed my fingers and tightened my fist until it glowed brightly. Everyone stared at my hand as I slowly peeled back my fingers to reveal a tiny, but brightly lit star.

"Whoah," Ayla breathed.

"Now make a wish," Archie told me.

"I wish to know everything I need to know about Rex Sullivan including, but not limited to: whether he is trustworthy, whether he is honest, and everything he has seen or heard concerning our current case," I told the star.

It seemed to shudder in my palm once, then twice. Then as if it had reconciled its purpose, it lifted itself up and flew directly at the vampire. The tiny star slammed into his chest with a ferocity that made me wince, exploding into streams of glittering light.

Within seconds, my head was filled with knowledge of Rex I hadn't had before. "We can trust him," I said with a nod.

Rex looked relieved.

"Why was he afraid of that?" Ayla asked, looking up at the adults. "That didn't seem very dangerous at all. So why would Rex sense danger from Astra?"

"Suppose Astra decided to wish that he explode in a thousand pieces?" Archie pointed out. "Or she wished that he would drop dead where he stood?"

"I wouldn't do that."

Archie clicked his beak. "But you could."

"But I wouldn't."

"But you could."

"Holy cow!" Ayla squealed. "Astra can grant wishes!"

CHAPTER ELEVEN

*Y*ou know how it goes in the movies, right?

Suddenly, the protagonist discovers an incredible power that changes everything. Everything! The sun comes out, the rain stops, the clouds part—everything, in a moment, gets more manageable. What had been challenging becomes no sweat, barely an inconvenience. The tide turns, the obstacles are obliterated—and on top of all that luck, riches rain down on the good guys as a reward.

Someone gets the guy or the girl at the end?

You know what I'm talking about.

So, that's not what happened here.

Ayla's excitement was mirrored by my other

two sisters who, no doubt, ran through a list of all of the things they wanted. Stuff out of reach because of money, or the limitations of magic, or my mother, suddenly seemed just around the river bend. It was this perfect moment sandwiched between hope and disappointment.

The disappointment came by way of a talking bird.

"That's not how it works. Astra can't grant wishes," Archie said with a chuckle. "She's not a genie. The goddess gave her a job, and the star power helps her do her job. So she can't just wish up a pony or a diamond bracelet or something." He rolled his wide eyes.

"Why not?" Ayla asked with a barely perceptible whine.

"It's like a computer issued for work. You're only supposed to use it for work. And I've seen it before. Athena's gonna lock that puppy in." He looked at me and cleared his throat. "Not to say the goddess doesn't trust you, but thousands of years dealing with human beings?" Archie tilted his head. "She doesn't like loopholes. You people always seem to find them."

I nodded. "So, I can only make a wish that assists me in a Star card case? Fair enough. I can work with that. Good to know, thanks."

"What do you mean, fair enough? That is not fair. It's the exact opposite of fair!" Ayla complained before Archie could even respond. "We're supposed to help the humans as priestesses, right? Well, think of all the things that Astra could do if she could grant whatever wishes she wanted to!"

Ayla handled herself so well in a previous case I sometimes forgot how young she was. "Ayla, I'm not a priestess, remember?"

"Well, I don't work for the police department, and I still talk to ghosts for you." The thirteen-year-old pouted. "We are supposed to work together. It's just unfair. You don't give somebody a gift like that and tell them they can't use it."

"The goddess has her reasons, Ayla," my mother told my sister. Her tone of voice made it clear she considered the matter decided.

"But it's unfair."

"Little girl, war is unfair," Archie told Ayla, tilting his head. "Getting a house foreclosed on because a cancer patient couldn't work after chemotherapy. That's unfair. Having a car stolen and insurance not covering its replacement? Unfair. Blaming an owl for hunting rabbits— grossly, incredibly unfair. Hugely unfair. Totally wrong." Ayla rolled her eyes. "Not giving Astra the godlike power to cheat her way through the rest of her life?" he shrugged. "I gotta tell you. Not so unfair."

Ayla brooded. "Why wouldn't the goddess want this to be easy?"

"Gods? Wanting things to be easy?" Archie laughed so hard he fell over. "What mythology books, bibles, or fairy tales have you been reading? Really, sometimes, you people come out with the funniest observations. It makes me wonder if you pay attention to anything at all."

Aunt Gwennie, Ami, Althea, Rex, and I chuckled.

My mother and Ayla did not.

Neither did Emma, and she didn't look happy about it. "I can tell that owl has a whole lot to say, and I never get to hear his answers for myself." Emma leaned forward and focused intently on Archie. "You think my being able to understand him would help with the case? Maybe your goddess would allow that wish."

"Oh, come on! So she gets to make a wish? She's a human! She's not even a witch!" Ayla complained. My youngest sister put her face in her hands, and I watched her shoulders heave in frustration. "I never get to have any fun."

"Ayla Arden, you may be a young priestess, but

you're still a priestess. Your behavior is unbecoming." Ayla shot daggers from her eyes at my mother's criticism. "Don't take that tone with me, young lady."

"What tone? I didn't say anything."

"You and I both know exactly what you were thinking." Althea had her hand on Ayla's arm, and Ami stood on the other side, patting the resentful young woman on the shoulder. They both silently tried to convince the youngest Arden sister to rein in her attitude, but it didn't look like it was working. "Listen to your sisters."

"Whatever. They didn't say anything, either." Ayla cocked her head.

"Look, I'm sorry I caused all this family drama," I jumped in, hoping to take the focus from Ayla. "But Emma is right. It might be useful for her and Archie to be able to speak to one another." I extended my hand flat, concentrated on the palm, clasped my hand closed, and opened it quickly. The star twinkled at me. "I wish that Emma and Archie could speak to one another."

This time, the itty-bitty orb gave just one slight shudder and flew across the room, slamming into Emma right between the eyes. "Well, that hurt far less than I expected it to," she murmured and then shook her head as if to clear it. "I don't feel any different."

"You're not supposed to feel any different," Archie told her sarcastically. "You're just supposed to be able to hear my pearls of wisdom."

Emma nodded. "I can hear them just fine, though you don't sound anything like I thought you would sound." Emma turned toward me. "By the way, just in case he gets annoying—is there a way to turn the ability on and off?"

Archie looked offended. "Well, aren't you sugar and spice? It's okay if you don't like me now that you can hear me," the raptor told the detective in a cheerful tone. "Not everyone has good taste."

"OKAY, let's start figuring this stuff out." I headed toward a whiteboard Aunt Gwennie set up in front of the seating area in the living room with information about the case. My mother and Aunt Gwennie sat in their usual spots on the couch, while my sisters huddled together on the carpet. Emma and Rex sat together on the love seat with enough space for someone else between them. Apparently, that distance would take a little while to bridge. "It's getting late, and some of us will have to sleep tonight."

Emma got up and joined me at the whiteboard. "So, this guy is in jail, and he's the one Astra has to keep alive." The detective reached back and tapped the picture. "His name is William Fisher; he's in his early forties. He's married to Gloria Fisher, and he works at the Barber Insurance Agency. The agency insured a painting called *Sunrise*, and they claim it was stolen from the office by William Fisher." Emma tapped a picture of the painting.

"When they made the complaint, Detective, what proof did they offer?" my mother asked. "They would've had to provide evidence, wouldn't they?"

"They would, and they did." Emma nodded and pulled out her notepad. "Melinda Barber gave us security footage from inside the office showing the painting leaning against a wall at the end of business yesterday. At approximately eleven o'clock at night, Will Fisher's card was used to swipe into the building, and the following morning the painting was gone."

"What about the footage of Will taking the painting?" Althea asked. "If you could see the painting on the camera, you must've been able to see who took it."

"The camera pans the interior of the office, so no," Emma responded. "Whoever stole it knew the camera was pointed away, rushed in, and grabbed it. By the time the camera panned back to that area, it was gone."

"That's awfully convenient," I told the detective. "It also doesn't make any sense. Suppose you had a million-dollar painting sitting in an office in a not so great part of town. Would you pan the security camera away from it?"

"If I was intent on stealing the painting, sure," Emma pointed out.

I turned to Ami at the sound of cards being shuffled.

"It's the judgment card," she said, holding the card up face out and showing everyone. "I mean, it could be that he's been legitimately arrested because he stole a painting, but I don't get the sense that's what the card is saying." She turned the card and gazed at it like she was trying to spot a subliminal message in the art. "I'm getting the strong sense of reckoning for him. Will, I mean. Something he...he wasn't aware of that suddenly smacked him right in the face. And it freaked him out."

"That's...helpful," Emma said, her expression clearly communicating she wasn't at all sure how helpful Ami's observation was. "So, anyway, that's how Will Fisher wound up in jail."

"I went over to the office this morning after Gloria's reading, and the place wasn't really ready for customers to walk in," I told the group. "I mean, it looked like it hadn't been updated since the 1970s. Not much effort was put into the decor. Hardly anyone there. The signage on the outside was minimal at best. Phones didn't ring, no customers were there, hardly any employees. And the guy who helped me was named Charles Fisher. I could swear there was a resemblance between him and Will."

"Brothers?" Emma guessed.

"That was my first thought, but I asked him when he introduced himself, and he denied being related to Will." I pointed to the ashtray I brought down and placed on the coffee table. "I managed to filch that on my way out so I could read it."

"What did you get?" Emma asked.

"Not much, to be honest." I was a little embarrassed that everything happening this morning precluded me from finding anything useful. When no one spoke, I added, "I was a little distracted with everything going on."

More cards shuffling. "The sun reversed," Ami murmured. "I think Astra was depressed this morning about getting fired. Depressed, sad, out of sorts. It made it difficult for her to concentrate."

"Okay, everyone gets it," I told Ami.

"Oy, was she," Archie chimed in. "I actually had to give her a pep talk."

"They get it!" I told Archie harshly.

"My apologies again," Rex said, an embarrassed grimace flashing across his face briefly. "I depend quite a bit on my instincts to read people, and it's very easy to become paranoid when someone is a blank slate the way you are to me." The vampire met my eyes. "I will speak to the captain tomorrow and attempt to undo the damage."

"Don't bother," I said and then turned to Ami. "And by the way, we don't need commentary on every little thing from your cards," I told my sister with a pointed glare. "And I don't get depressed."

"Everybody gets a little depressed sometimes," Althea said. "It's nothing to be ashamed of, Astra. We know you're not superhuman."

"Um, she kind of is superhuman," Ami told

Althea with a smile. "I mean, we all are, really. Well, except for Emma."

"Thanks for that," the detective called out.

"I didn't mean it literally," Althea sputtered in frustration. "It was just an expression of—oh, never mind. I swear, Ami, you're just like Mom. Only without the years of pessimism."

Ami gave Althea a menacing look.

A look that did, in fact, look remarkably like one of my mother's menacing looks.

I cleared my throat. "Can we focus? Two people's lives are threatened, and the clock is ticking."

"Okay, we have the Barber Insurance Agency with Charles Fisher, Will Fisher, and owned by Melinda Barber," Emma said, writing their names in dry erase marker on the board. "Does anyone else work there I left off?" I shook my head no. "As far as the list Melinda Barber provided me, this is it for employees—but considering the turn this has taken, I want to make sure my information is accurate. We may want to double-check this with the state employment rolls."

No one spoke.

"Okay, moving on. So, over here we have Rex's friend Val—"

"Hold on. Why are you putting Val on the board?" Rex asked Emma, frowning.

"Because I think she might belong there. Okay, so hear me out. The Barber Insurance Agency has been in business for twenty-seven years," Emma said, turning around to face him. "If they are nothing more than money-laundering operation, they've been doing it for nearly thirty years without raising so much as an eyebrow from the police, banks, or regulators. So they're obviously good at what they do, right?"

Rex nodded.

"Suddenly, they're on the verge of getting exposed. How? Well, Astra got involved in this because Will's wife came for a reading, and the Star card flipped. So let's ignore the Star card for a minute and focus on the reading. That she came in for a reading? I suspect it means something's going wrong in her life and has been going wrong for some time. I would bet dollars to donuts people don't usually come in for a reading when everything is going good, and they're happy."

We all turned and looked at Ami.

"You're right. She was concerned about her husband," Ami explained. "He'd always been a drinker, and she'd suspected he was alcoholic for a long time. Will struggled with quitting, you know?" A few of us nodded. "Anyway, something changed recently, and it scared her."

"Did it now," Emma murmured smugly.

"Gloria said Will's drinking expanded exponentially. What had been a couple of daily drinks turned into a daily bottle. He would come home and not speak to her, just sit in his wing chair downing whiskey. She said he seemed angry even though he wasn't an angry man. She didn't know what to do, and he wouldn't tell her what was wrong."

"And when did this escalation start?" Emma asked (as if she already had figured out the answer.)

"She said things changed the week after her birthday, which was…" Ami looked up, trying to remember the date. "It was the week after July fourth. July seventh or eighth, I believe."

"It's the last week in August, so that's about—"

"A month and a half," Rex whispered, staring at Val's name on the whiteboard. "I got the call the week after July fourth, as well. From Amadeus Bozeman." Rex pulled out his cell phone and scrolled through his history. "It was July tenth, I'm sure of it."

"That's what I thought. This?" Emma pointed toward the painting. "And this?" Emma pointed to Val's name. "My spidey-sense tells me whatever we're dealing with started the week after July fourth and that all of this is linked somehow."

"But how?" Aunt Gwennie asked.

"I don't know, but it has to be. It's too much of a coincidence. The dates. Rex, Astra, and pitting them against each other. Amadeus Bozeman and his phone calls and advice and his representation of Will Fisher while palling around with Melinda Barber. A paranormal goddess's interest in it all." The detective slapped her hand against the whiteboard. "These aren't two separate things. This is one big conspiracy."

Ayla turned to my mother and pointed at Emma. "Are you really sure she's not a witch?"

EVERYONE WAS ASSIGNED A DIFFERENT JOB.

Rex would contact vampires he knew had been close to Val, hoping we could paint a better picture of her life just before she was murdered. Aunt Gwennie would contact friends in Paranormopolis to see what she could uncover about Amadeus Bozeman and his banishment. Finally, my mother would go into a trance and visit the astral plane to find hints of what the people involved were trying to hide.

"Do you think you can find Val's ghost?" I asked Ayla.

"I know vampires can turn into ghosts if they want to. I met one once. But finding a specific ghost that didn't die in Forkbridge?" she sighed and rolled her neck. "If I can do it, it's not gonna be easy. And I think vampires get a lot of different options when they die, so Val may not even be a ghost."

I had no idea what that even meant.

"Do what you can," Althea said. "I'll let you know what I find on the internet." She looked at Emma. "My research would go much faster with your database access, you know."

Emma pulled out her police laptop, opened it, and plugged it in. "I need to charge my laptop before I can use it. So I'm just gonna leave it here. It'll be out of your way, right?" She leaned over and typed her password in. Then she quickly turned away.

"You're becoming quite the rule-breaker, Detective Sullivan," I said with a raised eyebrow.

"I'm trying to solve a case using a coven of witches, my vampire brother, and a talking owl, Astra. I feel like we jumped the shark quite a while ago on the concept of rule-breaking." She let out an exasperated sigh. "Besides, this has gotten so tied up in the paranormal I can't even begin to figure out how I would take this information to a prosecutor, anyway. Or explain it to another detective that didn't know about any of this."

"I gotcha."

"All I know is two people's lives are in danger, and if some goddess doesn't want Will Fisher dead? It makes me think that he's not guilty of what they claim. The question is why they're claiming it and what that claim is trying to hide." Emma raised her eyebrow. "What do we do if the guilty party is paranormal? Do you guys have, like, a paranormal police department or something?"

We did, once. I hadn't been keeping up with Paranormopolis and its new government, so I didn't know how to answer Emma's question. "I'll talk to Aunt Gwennie and see if she can find out. I don't really know anything. I've been gone a while."

Emma nodded. "Well, you have a goddess on your side, so I suppose she could help us out. Gods are big on punishment, or so I've read."

"I still don't know if I believe any of that. I just

say *Athena* because it's easier. That's what Archie claims, and that's what my mother believes, so I go along with it because, you know, it's just easier not to get into a disagreement every time they mention it."

Archie rolled his eyes and stared up at Emma. "I love it. She oozes stars from the palms of her hand like some kind of galactic nebular woman but, you know, it couldn't possibly be a gift from the goddess."

Emma laughed. "If you ever get a superhero name, it has to be that. Galactic Starwoman. Able to read large ashtrays with a single swipe."

"You appear to be in a much better mood," I observed to Emma, hitching my chin toward Rex.

Her brother stood across the room, away from everyone. He stared out the window silently. In fact, if someone was shooting a movie and told him to pose as the depressed, forlorn sexy male lead looking off into the distance? He probably couldn't have done a better job.

"I am."

"Don't want to kill him anymore?"

"Well, Ayla was right. He's already dead. So I can't kill him." Emma leaned on the back of the couch, her hands on her thighs. "I realized something in the last hour as we talked. Well, as I talked," she said with a grin. "Maybe I should've realized it before. But he's not the same person he was when I knew him as a human."

I stepped closer to listen.

"You all are very, very different from humans. Like, at first glance, you seem just like the rest of us. You just have some different abilities and some different beliefs; it's no big deal. That's what I thought, anyway. But the longer I know you all, the more I see that's not quite true."

I frowned. "What do you mean?"

"There's a whole aspect of the world you understand that I don't. And you've grown up accepting that as reality, whereas I can't even see it. Assuming that you see the world like me?" Emma shrugged. "It's not fair to you. It keeps me from knowing who you really are and getting the benefit of your perspective."

I thought about her words for a moment and then nodded. "Okay. I can see that."

"I've been working really hard to see Rex as my brother. The same guy I always knew. The same little boy that I followed around hoping he would let me play with him, pay attention to me. But he's not, is he?" She turned and looked at her brother. "Sure, that history is still there, but I realized I've tried to ignore that he was a vampire

—and yet being a vampire is who he is." Emma looked back at me. "He may even be more of a vampire than he is my brother, at this point. But I don't really know, because I've ignored that part of him as much as I could, so it wouldn't interfere with our relationship."

"And so you don't really know him right now."

"I don't. Or his life. I mean, I've changed, too. Being a soldier changed me. Being in Afghanistan changed me. Becoming a police officer changed me. Meeting you changed me. And Rex has talked to me about all of those changes." Emma looked embarrassed. "But I asked him not to talk to me about the vampire thing. About the mob thing. About what happened to him as a vampire. Sure, he'd tell me about Paranormopolis and stuff like that, but nothing personal. Nothing that he'd done."

"Because you asked him not to," I pointed out.

"Yeah, that's just it. I think maybe that was the wrong call on my part. Maybe that wasn't fair of me." Emma sighed. "How could I understand why he did what he did to me if I don't understand the nature of vampires? Your aunt understood. Your mother understood. They knew more about my brother and how he would react to what you were going to do to him than I did."

I smiled. "You didn't like that."

"No. I didn't like that," she agreed. "And before I blow my stack and scream at him for what he did to me, I need to take some time to understand why he did what he did. Part of that is letting him tell me who he is. And being willing to hear it."

I was impressed with how far Emma seemed to have come in such a short time. It was one of the things that so impressed me about the detective. How quick her mind was, how quickly she processed things, and how fast she could make a change when she realized she was going in the wrong direction.

Emma stood up. "I'm still gonna smack the hell out of him for lying to my parents, though." She snorted. "Allergic to the sun. What a lazy lie to tell."

CHAPTER TWELVE

"*A*re you sure you want me to come?" Rex asked from the backseat. The three of us sat in Emma's Malibu watching Melinda Barber's home for signs of nefariousness. Despite the late hour—ten at night, which, in Forkbridge was pretty darn late—bright lights shone from the windows, and shadows moved within the home.

"You have come. This is as far as we're going for the moment. I'm well aware that you're marked for death again. I need your big ears." Emma looked at her brother in the mirror, her slender fingers still gripping the steering wheel. "I'd have to get a warrant to tap their phones or bug their office. But you can hear what they're talking about, right?" Emma pointed toward the house. "You can hear any conversations going on in there?"

"Hold on a second. Is this legal?" I asked her before Rex could answer.

Emma turned toward me, her eyes hard and unblinking. "Really? Are you concerned about following the spirit of the law all of a sudden, ye old witchy thief of insurance agency ashtrays?"

I stared into Emma's bemused eyes. "We don't know the guilty party is paranormal. All we have are suspicions at this point. Suspicions and odd coincidences. If you have to submit this evidence to the human court, I'd think we'd want to make sure that we—well, you—do everything by the book."

Her snort had a sharp quality, like a horse that had been startled. "It's a third-degree felony in the state of Florida to record a conversation without all parties' consent. So yeah, that's a big deal evidence-wise, but we're not recording the conversation. I'd also like to point out we're pretty well off book. There's no book for this." Emma looked in the mirror again. "Still waiting on that answer, brother dear."

"I can hear the conversations. A woman and a man are talking," Rex told her. The vampire's voice was low and raspy. "They're arguing about

Will Fisher, whether he'll keep his mouth shut now or more steps need to be taken."

"Well, that was easy," Emma said, turning all the way toward the backseat. "Your hearing is really that good, huh?" Rex held up his finger, his eyes unfocused. "I love it when they're talkative," the detective whispered to me with a wink.

"The man said, 'Are you sure we can trust him?' and slammed his hand down on something wooden. Perhaps a table. The woman answered, 'No, Jerry. I'm not.' And he responded, 'Then why are we even doing this?'" Rex said, repeating the conversation he was overhearing.

"Wait a minute. Who's Jerry?" I whispered. Emma shrugged.

Rex continued, "You heard what I said: 'the woman responds' to Jerry. Then she says, 'He told the police that he has a witness. He's not going to stop digging until all of us are in jail.' The man just sighed, 'You know what they say about vengeance. It's a dish best served cold, but it's better to not serve it at all. Especially when there are vampires involved. I'm not getting drained,' he tells her."

"Did you say vampires with an *S*? More vampires?" I turned and looked at Rex. "Are there any other vampires in Forkbridge? Besides you, I mean."

"Do you know how many witches there are in town?" Rex arched his eyebrow, his expression calmly detached.

"No, but I don't really care who else is here. Aren't you vampires territorial or something?"

"No, that's a myth," he responded.

"You know, Astra, if this Amadeus Bozeman dude is as potentially dangerous as you say, maybe you should start to care who's running about this town," Emma said. She stared stubbornly through the window at the house and then shrugged. "Anyway, Rex, you didn't answer. Can you sense other vampires? Are there any more here?"

"Not that I'm aware of, but no, my ability to sense another vampire in the area is fairly limited. And I wouldn't be able to sense anyone else at all if they're in the ground." The calm inscrutability wrapped Rex in a sheen of untouchability that I wish I could learn without becoming a blood-sucking parasite. "Again, we are not territorial, and we don't tend to attack one another."

"That would make a real mess, huh?" Emma

shuddered. "In the ground?" she asked. "What does that mean?"

"If their lair is below the surface. The earth acts as protection for us in more ways than one. If the vampire was underground, I wouldn't be able to hear so much as a whisper of their existence even if I stood above the spot they hid in." The vampire's fangs peeked from between his lips, the only outward indication he was something other than human. "As to your question before—do we know who Jerry is?"

"No." The detective studied the house. "There are two vehicles in the driveway, though, and as far as I'm aware, only one person lives there," Emma said, tapping her fingers against the steering wheel. "Let's check out who owns them."

One car was a standard sedan, metallic blue and conservative. The other was a white van with no windows that wouldn't have looked out of place on a kidnapping episode of *Law and Order*. It had no markings or company names on the side.

Emma pulled out her tablet and tapped license plate numbers into a police app. "That one belongs to the Widow Barber," Emma said, pointing to the sedan.

"Widow?" I asked.

"Yeah, I may have forgotten to mention it, but her husband died about four years ago. Gerald Barber. Heart attack. He was the original owner of the Barber Insurance Agency." The screen lit up Emma's face, and I glanced toward the house to make sure no one was watching. "Huh. That van? It's registered to a Gerald Sandor." She looked up. "I've never heard of a Gerald Sandor."

"Jerry?" I guessed.

"That's a Hungarian name. Well, the surname," Rex murmured. "In English, the name would be Alexander. Gerald is not a Hungarian name, however."

Emma looked up. "How do you know that?"

"Hungarian names are quite popular with vampires. Many of them translate their names to the Hungarian equivalent for use in the human world. So I've come across a lot of them."

"You didn't," Emma pointed out.

"I didn't," he agreed but didn't elaborate.

"I'm just curious," I said, leaning over to glance at the tablet. "What was Gerald Barber's middle name?"

Emma squinted at the screen. "Let's see here. They don't list middle names in this database. Just the last name." She tapped the corner of the screen rapidly. "Let me look somewhere else. Give me a second."

"Barber is definitely not a Hungarian name," I mentioned.

Rex shook his head. "I don't believe so, no."

"I think it's French." I tried to remember what little I knew about surnames. "I knew some French witches at the Academy and, like, three of them were named Barber."

"Okay, here we go," Emma said, tapping something on the tablet. "Gerald Alexander Barber." The detective looked up, her eyes alight with wide-eyed fascination. "Okay, shot in the dark here, but are you telling me Melinda Barber's deceased husband is a freaking vampire?"

As if it was scripted, the door of Melinda Barber's home flew open just as Emma's observation echoed in the car. "Get down!" she whispered, and the three of us slunk low in our car seats.

Jerry stormed out and stomped toward the van. Then, after a rough jerk on the door, he climbed into the driver's seat and started it with an aggressive race of the engine.

I looked at the time on my phone. It was eleven-thirty. "Where is he going this late at night?" I whispered.

The three of us watched him back out of the driveway with a lot of engine noise and a bit of tire squealing. Then he took off toward town.

"This isn't late for vampires. If he is a vampire, this is right before lunchtime," Rex whispered back.

"We're going to follow him," Emma announced. "If we're lucky, he'll lead us to the safe house." She started the car and pulled quickly into the street, heading after the white van. "I mean if there is a safe house. Which there must be. Amadeus Bozeman has to be meeting with the vampire somewhere. Right?"

We followed the van through the streets of Forkbridge. The homes stood silent, and most windows were dark. Most of Forkbridge appeared to be home asleep, and I wondered again how Rex Sullivan was planning to make money in this town from a dance club. "Why are you opening a dance club?" I asked the vampire.

"You want to talk about this now?" Emma asked.

"Just something I was curious about, that's all. It just seems ill-advised." I pointed at the homes. "This isn't a 'close down the bar' kind of place. The whole town's already in bed, and the local news isn't even over."

"There are only a limited number of businesses I can run, considering I'm only able to manage them after sundown and before sunrise. That was one of them."

"If you want a physical business, I guess. But, still, I can't help but think it was an ill-advised business to put your money in," I told Rex over my shoulder. I pointed again. "This place rolls up the carpets at nine every night. Including Saturdays."

"It won't depend on Forkbridge business. The club can be seen from the highway, the one that runs between Cassandra and Orlando," Rex said, referencing the famous psychic town next to Forkbridge. "This place has never capitalized on that traffic, and there's only that one bed-and-breakfast there. I feel a dance club would be relatively safe for me to own openly and could be quite lucrative with the right promotion. The number of people passing Forkbridge on the highway per night is substantial."

Emma nodded distractedly, but as we

approached the on-ramp, I could see from the corner of my eye she wore an expression of concern.

"He's speeding," Emma murmured. I could feel the tension building in her body as an almost imperceptible buzz of anxiety. I was wrong. I'd love to say the tension and expression were concern, but nope. She was always hoping she'd get to open up her Malibu and zip through the town like the speed demon she was. "Just a little bit, though," she muttered, disappointed.

I chuckled. "Try and dial back your dissatisfaction, there, Speed Racer."

"Hey," she shot me a look and swallowed down any further comment.

"Sorry." I faced forward again and sat up straighter. "Your driving skills are substantial. I will give you that. And I know you don't get to run the Malibu through her paces enough. Though, you know, we can just go to a racetrack on a Saturday when you're off and make it go in circles really, really fast. They have that now. We don't have to constantly hope the bad guys will run away."

"It's all right. You can laugh. I know I deserve it." The remaining tension left her body, and I heard the smile in her voice. "Yeah, I'm a little bit obsessed with my car."

I couldn't help but smile back. It was good to have my relationship with Emma rubber-band back to normal. Well, normal for us, anyway. "Sorry. I will endeavor to mask my amusement."

"How much longer are we going to follow him?" Rex asked.

If Rex would just go back to where he came from, it would be perfect.

"Until we find out where he's going, or we lose him," Emma told her brother.

The Malibu's speedometer approached seventy miles per hour, and Rex frowned with unmistakable disapproval. "Can you slow down?" the vampire asked. "You're going ten miles over the speed limit."

"Why?" Emma frowned back at him for even suggesting such a thing. "He's going seventy. You do remember I'm actually a cop, right?"

"Does that mean you can get away with speeding?" I asked. Considering we had one of two people I had to keep alive in the car with us, I was somewhat on Rex's side here. Emma was a great driver, but we were dealing with a lot of unknowns.

"Yes. Obviously, it means I can get away with

speeding." Emma shot me that sideways look of challenge she got so often in my presence. Then she sighed. "I can get stopped for speeding, though, if the patrolman doesn't recognize my car. So maybe you're right. If we got pulled over, we'd lose him." She reluctantly let her foot off the gas pedal slightly.

"Have you really never wrecked this car?" Rex asked from the backseat.

"I am completely offended by the question," she told him with mock indignation. Emma slowed the car down to the speed limit and pressed her lips together in a frown. "Hmm. He's heading south." The detective frowned. "Rex, isn't he heading toward your construction site?"

There was a pause before he answered. "Yes."

We pulled onto the highway access road just in time to see the white van pull onto a dirt road. The gigantic sign announcing the construction of Sanguine loomed right next to it. "He's trespassing," Rex murmured.

"Not really. Well, I guess it depends on what land you own. It looks to me like it's right before the construction site." Emma parked her Malibu a half-mile from the dirt road and pulled her tablet out. "Yeah, no, you don't own that road. He's taking this path here." She pointed. "It goes toward the river running just behind your property."

"Have you been down there?" I asked Rex.

"No," he answered me. "I've not explored everything on my property. We have the permits to clear the wooded area from the river headwaters to the east. I've been keeping tabs on it since I purchased it, but I haven't had a chance to explore it all."

I glanced over at Emma. "Well, the guy who may or may not be a vampire is now beelining to the same tributary you're building your club near —so maybe the construction and club really are linked to this conspiracy somehow." I looked at Rex. "Who picked the spot to build?"

"I approved the location, but if pressed, I would have to admit I didn't much care where it was. Bozeman made the suggestion."

"Okay, this map says there's a dirt road, and then there's a bridge, then you drive down a little way, and there's kind of a plateau out over the river." Emma scratched her head. "It's a nice piece of property and all, but this property over here next to it?" she pointed to the dirt road on the map. "It's just the road and a strip at the back toward the river."

"If I was a suspicious person, I would say that

club would be a fantastic way to hide the comings and goings of people to whatever's built on that back land by the river," I told them both. "Who owns that property?"

Emma tapped her screen. "Miranda Barber."

"What on earth is going on here?" I asked no one in particular.

"Do we go take a look?" Rex asked.

"Not you. For all I know, that's where you die," I said, pulling out my phone. "Let me get some air support. Let's find out what we're walking into. Then we'll decide who goes. If anyone."

Rex, Emma, and I were waiting by the car for Archie to make his appearance. Once he arrived, we asked him to fly a mile or so into the property, check everything out, and then return to the car to tell us what he saw.

"You called me out here for this? You can't just walk down there? You're a vampire, you're a witch, and you have a gun," he said with a weary annoyance.

"None of us can fly," Rex pointed out.

"You're about as useful as an ashtray on a motorcycle," Archie snapped grumpily at the vampire. "What are you even doing here? I thought we decided you were a jerk? You don't get to ask me for help, fang-face."

"Archie, knock it off," I told the owl. Rex's Star card didn't change Archie's dislike and mistrust of the vampire at all. "Just get it done, could you?"

"People like him are the reason the gods don't bother talking to you people anymore. You know that, right?" Archie snapped with a scowl of distaste. "You people, too. You forgive too easily. For all you know, this idiot is the reason all this is happening."

I crossed my arms. "So, should I let Rex die even though Athena wants him to live? Maybe you want me to stake him myself? How would your goddess feel about that, do you think?" Archie glared at me sullenly. "We have a job to do, Archie."

An unpaid job.

Peering into his eyes, I watched them get wider, his pupils flicking to and fro as he looked for an argument he could make. Finally, he gave a hooting sigh. "Fine. You got me there. But I don't have to like any of this." He flew off into the sky, muttering.

After a few moments, the vampire said, "I don't think your owl likes me very much."

"I told you, he's not my owl. He's not a pet. But no, he doesn't like you very much. In case you were wondering, I also don't like you very much. Your sister has to love you." I jerked my chin toward Emma. "Thankfully, I just have to tolerate you."

The moonlight rippled across Rex's face. His lips, so red next to his pallor, shifted in a bemused smile. Then, just as the vampire was about to respond, Archie reappeared, landed on the car with a screech of his talons. "I saw a small concrete building with no windows and a heavy door. The white van is camouflaged under some branches next to it, but it's not that good."

"The camouflage?" I asked.

Archie nodded. "Further in toward the river, there's another building. A small cabin. I flew over it. The roof has holes in it, and there are no windows left, so I think it's old and falling down with nothing much in it. The inside walls have been removed or knocked down or were never there, I don't know."

"So there's an old house falling down and a new concrete building too small to live in?" Emma asked. Archie nodded. "Did you see anyone walking around?"

"I don't know for sure the first building is

new, but it was pretty clean. But, naw, no one was out and about. Could be someone in that little concrete box, but without windows?" He held his wings out and shrugged. "I couldn't tell you."

"Well, if the van's parked next to the small building, that's what we want to find out about," I told the assembled sleuths. "I don't think that old, decrepit house matters much. If it's concrete with no windows, though, getting in it might be tricky."

"We also can guess that the vampire's sitting in the center of the box, right?" Emma guessed. "I mean, with no windows and thick concrete walls? That's his lair, right?"

"Say it is. Why would he go back there this early?"

Emma looked at me and shrugged. "A nap?"

"Vampires do not nap," Rex told his sister with an expression of something akin to horror. "We have only half the day to move about. We would not return to our lair until close to sunrise."

"Well, does anybody else have any ideas?" I asked. My question was met with silence. Then I yawned. "Well, I'm not comfortable running to a vampire's lair and knocking on the door in the middle of the night. Color me cautious."

"That's a wise choice," Rex murmured.

"Hey, look, don't get me wrong. I'll do it if I have to, and I could handle it just fine," I told the vampire indignantly. "But your sister is a human, and I've heard some horror stories about humans that get too close to vampire lairs."

"We have more information than we started with," Rex said. "Maybe we should head back to Arden House and see what everybody else discovered, pool the information, and decide where to go next."

"Sounds good." Emma nodded and moved toward the driver's door.

"Is he coming?" Archie asked, pointing to the vampire with scornful resentment.

I snapped my fingers toward the bad-tempered owl. "Give it a rest, bird."

"And get off my car, Scratchy!" the detective told him.

CHAPTER THIRTEEN

*A*yla raced up to me before all three of us were through the door. As she sped through the hallway, she turned her head from side to side, scanning each face for some indication we were about to speak. When we didn't, she did.

"I can't find his friend anywhere," my sister gasped like she'd just finished a marathon. "I was so confused that I had Althea look for records on her because, you know, sometimes vampires create human records for themselves?" Ayla looked at Rex, and he nodded. "So, like, we found her records, and they kind of end here in Forkbridge?"

"That makes sense," Rex said. "Amadeus told

me she was killed here. It's the main reason I returned."

"Wait a minute. That's the main reason you returned?" Emma asked, her eyebrow arching.

"Right, so, anyway, I tried to call her ghost, and nothing happened which, you know, isn't exactly that out of the ordinary because it's tough to find ghosts once they move on, and I don't even know how difficult it would be to—"

"Ayla, take a deep breath and try to calm down. Your thoughts are racing, and so is what you're telling us." I put my hands on my younger sister's shoulders. "Try to organize your thoughts, take a deep breath, calm yourself, and explain the important points of what you're trying to tell us. But slowly. We don't need to know what you did that didn't work unless it's important."

It was like watching a puppy walk its first steps: awkward, and then before you know it? That thing is running and jumping and climbing and fetching, tumbling keister over cauldron with excitement.

"She's trying to tell you she cannot find the dead vampire in the great beyond," my mother explained, walking up to us. She reached over to pull Rex through the door and then closed it firmly. "What's more, the dead she and I have both spoken with saw Valeria Scott in Forkbridge several days before the paperwork was submitted to transfer her assets, but never the day of and never again after that."

"What do you mean by transfer her assets?" Emma asked.

"Her entire human-held fortune was transferred to the Barber Insurance Agency. We won't know about her fortune in Paranormopolis until the morning."

"You mean to be managed by them?" Rex asked, confused.

"No, I mean to keep," Mom said, her brow wrinkling. "Well, more specifically, the assets were transferred to Miranda Barber. Some of the money remained with the woman individually. Some of it was transferred into the coffers of the insurance agency. But it was all, in one way or another, transferred."

"How did you find this out?" Emma asked my mother.

"Althea hacked their bank accounts!" Ayla told the detective excitedly, her eyes sparkling. "We got to look at all the transfers, and we could see—"

"Ayla, Emma is still a detective, so we don't really want to tell her when we break the law in quite so explicit terms." Ayla's expression dropped in the face of my admonishing glare. "Relax, I'm sure it's fine."

"Are you?" Emma asked. "Hacking a bank is literally a federal offense, you know."

"Oh, for the goddess's sake, I didn't hack a bank," Althea announced as she joined us in the front hallway. "I hacked a bank account login, and hacking is an overblown word for what happened. Rex showed me the check he got from the insurance company earlier, I took a chance they used ridiculously easy passwords, and I got lucky. That's all. Miranda's login is her name, and her password is password123."

"That is technically hacking a bank, Althea, but since that woman made it so easy for you, I'm gonna let it slide. She practically held up a sign saying 'hack me.' Jeez," Emma leaned against the wall. "Since you got in anyway, what did you find?"

"Well, her login has access to both the business bank accounts and her personal bank accounts. There's a lot of money shuffling back and forth between them, but that's not even the weird part. I figured out what happened with Val's assets because there's an electronic check in Miranda's personal bank account," Althea explained. "It's to the IRS, and it's marked 'gift tax.' It was paid into Valeria's tax account from Miranda's checking account, and it was for almost sixteen million dollars."

"Miranda paid sixteen million dollars in tax? For Val?" Rex asked.

Althea nodded. "Out of a sudden influx of almost a half a billion dollars. I looked up how much of a gift that would cover, and the amounts match pretty closely."

"Miranda Barber has half a million dollars?" Emma asked with a dazed expression. "In her personal account?"

"Not half of a million. Half of a billion, with a *B*," Althea clarified. "About four hundred million dollars was transferred to Miranda Barber a month and a half ago. Roughly, anyway. I'd have to look at the exact date. She immediately wrote two checks; one to the insurance agency as an owner investment, and another to the IRS to cover Valeria's gift tax on the transfer."

"It really is as if Val gave her entire fortune to this woman," Emma said, looking at Rex. "But why would she do that?"

Rex waved his hand. "Not possible. She spent lifetimes building up her assets to ensure she would have enough to live a life in the human world without being detected. There's no way she would just hand all of what she had over to some woman in Florida she never even mentioned. It's completely against everything she ever taught me."

"Maybe she had a will, and they have directives on how to distribute the money?" I asked.

"We checked; there is no will on file. No probate case. And you don't pay gift taxes on inherited money," Althea told me. "Paperwork-wise, it looks like Valeria Scott chose, for whatever reason, to simply hand her entire liquid fortune over to Miranda Barber. No explanation, no note, but enough legal paperwork to make it look like a choice."

"Liquid fortune?" I asked. "What does that mean?"

"Just the cash moved. Val owned a variety of properties in locations worldwide, and none of those have been transferred. Including a house here in Forkbridge, which, presumably, would have been easy to do." Althea crossed her arms. "Now, I could be wrong that it's all her cash—Val was a vampire, and I'm sure she's got a Swiss bank account with tons of money in it, right?"

"Probably," Rex agreed.

"But as far as I can tell? Val's cash accounts in the United States have been emptied out and dumped into Miranda Barber's account, all earmarked as a gift."

WE ALL WORKED WELL into the night searching databases, googling property records. The case of the arrested insurance agent's stolen painting had exploded so far outside its initial boundaries it was challenging to narrow down which path was the most promising. Then, as two in the morning approached, my mother looked up, frowning. "Astra, where's Rex?"

"What?" I asked distractedly. I looked up from Althea's laptop and the pages of newspaper articles I'd been scanning. "Sorry, Mom, what did you ask me?

"I asked where Rex was. He's not here."

That got everyone's attention. Five witches and one detective sat straight up—all looking off in a different direction like we'd coordinated a search grid beforehand. The sixth and youngest witch shrugged.

"Maybe he's in the bathroom," Ayla said with a yawn.

"He's a vampire, dimwit," Althea told Ayla. "They don't go to the bathroom. Don't you read the creature lore books you're assigned?"

"Althea, don't call your sister names," Aunt Gwennie told Althea distractedly, her eyes scanning the house. "They sneak up so silently. I suppose they can leave just as silently."

"What can?" Ayla asked.

"Vampires."

"You don't suppose he figured out what was going on and went to go deal with it on his own in some sort of stupidly chivalrous suicidal mission of epic idiocy, do you?" Emma asked no one in particular. Finally, Ami got up silently from the table, her face worried. "I mean, he knows that your Greek goddess Star card thing is no joke, right?"

"He's your brother, Emma. You know him better than I do." I rubbed the back of my neck, which was knotted with tension. "Would he do that?"

"Would he do that," Emma murmured the words like a statement, and she thought about it for a moment. "If he thinks he fell into something —like an idiot—that got his friend Val killed? Yeah, I think he might not be thinking straight. Or I just don't understand how vampires think, which is more than likely the case" The detective threw down the papers. "Dammit, Rex."

"Look, he may be fine—"

"Right, Astra, the Star card flipped over on my vampire brother who's in the middle of a gigantic conspiracy involving four hundred million dollars, another vampire, possibly yet another vampire, a crazy backstabbing witch, and he just snuck out of the house to get coffee in the middle of the night without telling anybody," she spat at me, her tone challenging. "At two in the morning. Alone."

"Look, Emma, I'm not saying you're wrong—"

"Oh, good. Because for a second there, I thought about taking your advice and just laying down for a nap."

I blinked. "Um, I didn't give you any—"

"You did. You said he's fine!" Emma slammed her fist on the table. "And what do I do if he's not, anyway? This is all so far beyond me it may as well be in Greek!" She shoved the vampire books away and crossed her arms. "How am I supposed to help anyone in this case? There's no training for vampire suspects in the police academy! Hell, I have more training on dealing with alligators!"

Althea and Ayla stared wide-eyed at Emma. They were used to the detective being unflappable, and Emma was suddenly—obviously —flapped.

I stood up. "Get up," I told Emma.

"Why? Where are we going?"

My mother tried to intervene quietly. "Astra, perhaps we should—"

"Stay out of this, Mom. I've got this." I turned back to the detective. "We're going upstairs to my room," I told Emma. She still didn't move, so I reached down and pulled her out of her chair. "You need to change. Let's move."

Emma yanked her arm from my grip but stood up. "What the hell are you talking about?"

I knew Emma was worried. It was all over her face.

And, well, tumbling out of her mouth.

At high volume.

One of the most challenging parts of working on any case was keeping your emotions from getting out of control. When you're trained in law enforcement, you learn to do that. Other jobs have to tamp down on the feels as well—doctors, vets. So you keep the emotions that let you do the job, and you learn to squash down and ignore the ones that don't help.

Maybe not super healthy, but it's useful.

Anyway, all those things go out the window

when someone you love is involved. It's why doctors don't operate on family members or why vets have another vet for their own pets.

Emma was a fantastic detective, but her brother and his situation played havoc with her judgment and emotions.

And her confidence.

"This isn't my only uniform," I told her, pointing. "You're right; this case might involve several vampires, and that Jerry dude is definitely sketchy. I know there's nothing I'm going to be able to say to you that will keep you in this house—"

"Damn straight," she snapped, her eyes flashing angrily.

"—but what I can do is make you more prepared than you are right now," I continued. "My uniforms have certain defenses that will work on anybody wearing them. It doesn't matter that you're not a witch. I can make you bulletproof, and I can make you bite-proof, so let's go get changed."

Emma stared at me, her face tightening.

"Did you hear me? Let's go."

"Yep." She sniffed. "I heard you all right."

I arched my eyebrow. "Then what's the problem?"

"I cannot believe I'm just now finding out about this. You have more than one of those? Seriously? How could you not let me borrow the bulletproof bite-proof magical Black Widow outfit before this?"

I held out my hand. "Can I have your gun?"

Emma's hand flew protectively to her hip, her fingers spread over the firearm lovingly. "That's different. This is police issue, and it's—"

"Right. How about your spare down there?" I pointed toward her ankle. "That's your personal gun, right? Can I borrow it?"

She stared at me with pursed lips, like a judge about to pronounce a sentence. Then her eyes narrowed. "Fine. Point taken."

I WOULDN'T HAVE TAKEN Emma's big old Punisher gun—it was too big and heavy to deal with in a fight, and it wouldn't do much against a vampire, anyway. I hoped I'd made the point I was trying to get across, though—it was a big deal for me to let Emma borrow my outfit. Had the situation been different, we would've had a much longer conversation about it.

As it was, we didn't really have time.

I didn't even know how many benefits of the "Black Widow" outfit I'd just given Emma would work on humans, but I was sure it would keep her alive. The vampire protection was nothing more than a gigantic shield, and it should work on anyone wearing it.

Emma pulled her hair into a ponytail, then pulled out a pair of fingerless gloves and pushed them halfway up her forearm.

"What are you doing?" I asked, pointing at the gloves.

"Covering up as much as I can." Emma continued to pull the gloves higher. "I figure you wear the gloves for a reason. I doubt your bicep does a whole lot of psychic readings. I need to keep my fingers free, though." She picked up her gun off the wooden desk in my room and looked at the utility belt. Within seconds, a holster manifested. "Whoah. How did it know I needed one of those?" She placed the gun in the holster and looked at herself in the mirror. "It's a little big."

"Give it a second."

"And it's really snug in the chest area," she told me. "You know, here"—she pointed to her chest —"and here"—she pointed under her arms—"are just incredibly tight." Emma tossed an amused glare over her shoulder. "It's so tight I almost can't breathe."

"Har har, very funny. I'm glad to see you're maintaining your sense of humor."

"I used to tell the funniest jokes right before firefights in Afghanistan," Emma admitted as she pulled the ponytail tight. "I don't know what it is about high-stress situations that just turns me into a sarcastic comedian, but that's my coping mechanism."

"Everyone has one."

"If I could do stand-up while someone shot at me? I'd probably make millions." Emma turned my full-length mirror toward her to look at herself from head to toe, then shook her head. "That's weird. It almost fits too well."

"It looks good on you."

Emma turned around and looked at her tight, armored backside in the mirror. "Wow. This thing fits like a second skin. My butt looks great."

"While we've been talking, it's been molding to the contours of your body. That's part of its magical properties—it fits the first time perfectly with no alterations."

Emma took a deep breath, screwed up her face, and pulled her arms over her head. "No, it fits great," she told me, suddenly pale as she stretched.

"You okay?"

Emma breathed deeply once more, then turned to meet my eyes. "Every time I think of my brother, I can't breathe. Like, it feels like the air doesn't have enough oxygen. I thought it was your magic outfit, but I don't think it is." She blinked back tears again. "What if we don't figure this out in time?"

"Emma, he'll be okay," I told her with much confidence. It wouldn't help her to coddle her fears or admit they were valid. Not at this point. "Remember, the Star card almost always gives me seventy-two hours. It just flipped a few hours ago. So whatever Rex might wind up walking into? It's probably not gonna be tonight."

The detective turned away from me quickly. I didn't see the following expression cross her face, but I sensed the deepening apprehension. I saw her shoulders rise as she took another deep breath, and I glanced in the mirror to spot another frown across her face. Then, when she caught me watching, she turned away again.

"Emma, we've got this."

"Do we?" Emma clenched her eyes shut and screwed up her face again for a moment. When she opened her eyes, her expression was determined and resolute. "Okay. Let's go find my brother."

"Okay," I said with a nod. I glanced out the window, hoping to see Archie, but he wasn't there. I dropped my eyes to the driveway. "We should take my Jeep."

Her head snapped up, and she put her hands on her hips. "You know I'm already off my game, and you want to take my car from me, too? Are you trying to piss me off, Astra?"

"No, but your brother might be," I told her, pointing down toward the front yard. "Your Malibu isn't where you left it."

The detective raced to the window and thrust herself through it.

"So we take my Jeep?" I asked again.

"If he's not dead when we find him, I'm gonna kill him," Emma proclaimed hotly. She turned from the window and stormed across the room toward her bag. "I can't believe he honestly thinks I don't have a tracker on her. She's the only thing I love more than my family. Idiot." Emma pulled out her tablet and tapped on the screen a few times. "Got him."

For once, I was grateful for Emma's car obsession. "Where is he?"

"At his construction site."

I nodded and reached out to grab the bottle of Grey Goose we'd snagged from the jail earlier. Then I crossed the room and grabbed the ashtray I'd filched and slipped it into my bag. I kept getting distracted and ignoring these two items, never finding time to read them. "I'll take these and read them once we're over there. We also need to stop by Will Fisher's house and just make sure he's home with his wife." I frowned. "I'm starting to feel like two Star cards is one too many."

Emma nodded. "We are relying an awful lot on the seventy-two hour clock ticking here. I hope we really can." She stepped toward the door. "Ready?"

"As I'll ever be."

CHAPTER FOURTEEN

$\mathcal{W}$ ill and Gloria Fisher lived in a modest home that resembled so many other ones in Forkbridge. The low-pitched roof of the single-story Mediterranean-style house was missing a few tiles at the edges. Still, the stucco walls were clean and looked recently painted. "I don't know what I was expecting," I told Emma as I pulled the Jeep into the cul-de-sac, "but it was something bigger or fancier than that."

"I just thought he was an insurance agent, so this was about what I expected when I showed up here. Nothing out of the ordinary in the house, either."

"You arrested him here?"

Emma nodded. "He wasn't at work. That was one of the reasons Barber claims to have suspected him first thing this morning."

"Do you still think this painting even exists?" I leaned back in the driver's seat, examining the house. The kitchen windows were lit, and light from the living room shone out onto the front yard. Before she could answer, I added, "I think they just made it up. Maybe Will Fisher found something out, and they needed leverage over him. What better way to get someone out of the way? Make a complaint something's gone that never even existed in the first place? They can't come up with it. We can't recover it."

"Or that small building behind my brother's site is an entrance to the type of place you can store a million-dollar painting along with a lot more stolen art." Emma yawned. "It would make sense. But let's just say you are right. There's no painting. This is just a way to shut Will Fisher up. Why? What does he know?"

"Well, I guess that's what we're trying to figure out, isn't it?" I opened the door. "Okay, five minutes. I have to make sure this guy is still alive. Let me see what I can see, and I'll come back in a minute." I got out of the car and closed the door before Emma could argue with me. Then, with a quick sprint, I ran toward the house and ducked down among the palmettos lining the front of the home.

I'd barely hidden myself in the bushes when I heard Gloria Fisher.

"Why didn't you tell me?" she wailed angrily, sobs choking her words, from somewhere within the house. She sounded close to where I hid crouched beneath the window, and my breathing got shallower. "They're going to kill us, Will. And now that you've told me, I'm going to go down with you! Why did you tell me? Isn't it better that I don't know?"

"I had to tell you because we have to run," Gloria's husband responded, his voice slightly slurred. "Bozeman says the police are gonna get me one way or another, and since I can't tell him what's going on, he doesn't have an outstanding defense for me. I've known him for years. He'd never lie to me." I heard a soft crash and then glass breaking. "Damn, sorry. I'm a little unsteady. I didn't mean to break that." Will burped.

Will Fisher thinks that Amadeus Bozeman doesn't know what's going on? I frowned. And what did he mean, he'd known the guy for years? What game was Bozeman playing here?

"You're unsteady? You're unsteady? You're an unsteady husband, you drunk! After all these years of marriage, after everything that I've put up with—how could you get involved in something like this? Something they could send you to jail for!" Gloria's voice combined hopelessness and rage. "You promised me when you took this job there was no way anyone could get hurt!"

"I didn't get involved!" Will hiccuped. "No one has gotten hurt! Gloria, get a hold of yourself!" There was another loud crash through the cracked window as if Will Fisher slammed into a table. "I told you no one would be hurt, and no one's been hurt. You're mad about this now, but you weren't mad about it when my job bought you this house."

"A house I am going to have to live in alone when you spend years in prison!"

I rose from my hiding spot just enough to peek into the house. Gloria and Will stood facing each other, Will was unkempt and disheveled, Gloria in a nightgown. A large half-finished whiskey bottle hung loosely from Will's fist.

"Do you really think I wanted to get involved?" Will actually sounded sincere. "I didn't want to get involved, but I have to support this family. I do what they tell me. I do it, and I knew something was off, but I never asked too many questions. I did what I had to do to take care of us, Gloria."

"So, it's my fault?" Impatience flashed across her face. "Is that what you're saying? It's my fault you and your brother chose the easy path?"

Will held up his hands. "No, of course not. Honey, that's not what I meant."

"Then, whose fault is it?"

Will glanced directly toward my window and pointed vaguely at it. I dropped down in the blink of an eye and held my breath, but it didn't seem as though he'd seen me. "Who do you think? Right now, today, it's my idiot brother. If he hadn't lost the paperwork, nothing would have come out, no one would have gotten hurt, and I'd still have my job, income, and my reputation."

"I don't think your reputation as the town lush has been damaged," Gloria spat viciously.

"Stop it. You know what I mean. I wouldn't have found what I found."

"I'm not the one that decided work in a

normal office wasn't enough," Gloria said quietly as if her anger had exhausted her. Like she had always been the voice of reason with her husband but now had no idea how to reach him. "You're the one that did that. I overlooked your drinking, your brother's greed, and his affair with your boss—"

I blinked. Miranda and Charles Fisher?

"—and none of us asked questions when Jerry died," Gloria said wearily.

"Crazy Jerry was a psycho that anyone in their right mind would want to do something about," Will told his wife. "No one asked questions because it was a solution to a problem we could all sympathize with. And if Charles did it for Miranda?" I rose up slightly and glanced in. Will held up his hands as if pleading with his wife. "Well, it might be the first thing I ever respected about my brother. None of us would be in this mess if Jerry didn't do what he did."

Gloria Fisher turned away as her husband spoke, and I ducked back down. Her voice, crestfallen, said, "You had to have known. I don't even know you, Will. You're disgusting."

"Oh yeah?" Will's voice edged with hysteria. "Well then, maybe you never should have married me, Gloria."

There was a crash from inside the house, and the next thing I knew, Will thundered onto the front walkway through the front door just five feet from my hiding spot. I dropped down quickly, flattening onto my stomach and pressing hard against the ground.

The faint light from the kitchen illuminated him with keys in hand, heading for his car, and I swallowed. The last thing this man should be doing is driving. So many things threatening the guy I was having trouble figuring out what I needed to defend him from—but alas, the drunken Will Fisher was going to drunk drive while in an emotional tailspin and wrap himself around a tree after a tongue-lashing from his wife.

Great.

I JUMPED IN THE JEEP, switched on the ignition, and spun the off-road wheels on the gravel as I took off after Will Fisher.

"What did I miss?" Emma asked calmly.

I related what I'd overheard hiding in the bushes as we raced west on Poplar Avenue. "So, Miranda and Charles Fisher are having a romantic affair, Jerry Barber is supposed to be dead, but might be a vampire, since we think he's driving a white van, and Amadeus Bozeman is up to something, because his own client thinks he can't confide in him," I finished, my eyes darting back and forth between the street and the rearview mirror. "And Will Fisher's known Bozeman for years somehow."

"Is he going toward the construction site, too?" Emma asked quickly, pointing down the side road Will turned on. "There's not much in that direction other than the site for Sanguine." She squinted out the driver-side window as the car turned. "I think he's on the phone."

I took one hand off the wheel, made a fist, and created a tiny star. "I want to hear both ends of that telephone conversation," I told it. The petite star shuddered and rose slightly. "Wait!" I yelled.

It halted its ascent and sort of...stared at me.

"Both of us. Emma and I both need to hear it," I added quickly.

It shuddered again. Then the star bounced as we hit a bump, using the momentum to fly forward through the front windshield and toward Will's car.

Within seconds, the Jeep filled with voices.

"I can't just go running with my wife. She won't go," Will Fisher snarled. "I told you both I'm not going to tell anybody! I don't care what you have down there, or what you're doing, or why you have it," he pleaded. "I just want—"

"I told you not to talk about this on the phone," the man responded, cutting him off. "Remember, we go down, you go down—and I'll find some way to take your shrew of a wife down with the rest of us, too. You're in the middle of a criminal case, you idiot. Your phone could be tapped!"

"What?" Will laughed. "No way. This is Forkbridge, not Chicago or New York. We don't even have a local judge! I might as well be in Podunk Springs for all the attention our little Opie-town gets from the police," Will told him, laughing. Loud smacking sounds echoed as if he was taking a drink, "They don't care enough to tap my phone, Chuckie. They only care because our boss made them care!"

"Are you drunk?" the man asked.

"Oh, brother mine, I am so drunk," Will admitted, chuckling. "I shouldn't be behind the wheel of this car right now. I shouldn't be going where I'm going. Maybe it'll be worse than what's going on now. But what else am I gonna do?" The drunken man suddenly sounded dejected, and his car in front of us slowed down. "You know what? I don't mind risking myself, but not Gloria. And not for a brother who would sacrifice my wife and me so easily. She doesn't deserve that."

"Uh oh," Emma muttered. "I've done enough interrogations to sense a change in the wind. And that, Astra, is a change in the wind."

A long moment of silence followed.

"What are you going to do?" the man I assumed was Charles Fisher asked his brother. His tone was menacing, coldly angry, and sociopathically unsympathetic to his brother's situation. It was a far cry from the bumbling insurance agent I met at the Barber Agency. "Right now, she only wants you in prison. So don't do anything that gets you and your whining wife dead."

Will's car abruptly stopped in the road. I hit the brakes and stopped far enough behind him I didn't think he would notice we were following him.

"Just forget about everything," we heard Charles tell Will.

There was a moment of silence. "No, I..." Will began, and then his voice trembled, "I'm not selling my soul to you, Charles. I want out. If it's you or me? Well, I'm not gonna lay down in a ditch and let you sacrifice us."

"You really think you can pull this off, you drunken idiot?" Charles's voice said, colder than a grave. "You think you can take me on? This is a plan years in the making. Years. You're not sober enough to make it through a day. This is not helping your wife, stupid. Not helping me, either. Will you just do exactly as I tell you? Or am I going to have to take you out of the equation?"

Just as Charles Fisher finished his threat, Will started the engine again and drove off down the highway access road toward Rex's construction site. After a few seconds, I let off the brake and accelerated.

"Hey, Chuck?"

"Yeah?" Charles Fisher asked gruffly.

"Only one way to find out if you're right about me."

Then the line went dead.

"You know, if the captain doesn't put you back on the payroll? I might pay you out of my pocket," Emma told me, her voice heartily impressed. "And I thought the bulletproof stuff was cool. That?" She pointed toward my hand. "That was the coolest thing I ever saw. Well, heard."

"Probably illegal," I pointed out.

"Did you illegally intercept communication without the prior consent of all parties to the communication?" Emma asked, her eyebrow arched. "Yes, technically, you did that. And yeah, it's technically a felony. But that usually only comes up when you try to use the tapes in a criminal case. We have no tapes, and we're not gonna do that, so it's not going to come up."

"You're the cop," I told her, shrugging.

"This is Forkbridge, not Chicago or New York," she responded, repeating Will Fisher's statement with a chuckle. "Besides, I was just sitting here in the car. I don't see any telephone interception stuff."

"Uh-huh. Keep justifying that corruption to yourself."

She held up her fingers about an inch apart. "It's just a little bit. A little tiny bit of itty-bitty corruption." We lurched to a stop as Will darted the car into a curve under the bridge right before the construction site to give him some time to pull ahead. While we waited, Emma's face hardened. "Look, we're doing it to help, and my brother's life is in danger. So, to be frank, all bets are off."

WILL TURNED AWAY from the half-built building and scanned the darkness looking for something...or someone. After a minute, he walked back over to the front of his car and took a cigarette out of his shirt pocket. Flipping his lighter, he lit the cigarette, leaned against the hood, and took another swig from the whiskey bottle, now only one-third full.

Emma and I hid behind a large excavator, watching.

"I know you're here," he shouted drunkenly. Will's voice echoed through the wood frames and masonry foundations haphazardly jutting up from the landscape like oddly planted trees. "Show yourself! I'm tired of this!"

"Can I help you?" Rex walked out from behind a temporary building. "You're trespassing, you know."

I stopped breathing as the two men I'd been charged with protecting walked toward one another. Rex's steps were sure, Will's haphazard and unsteady.

What if the two would attack each other?

What if there was some wild and

unpredictable confrontation looming that I needed to stop?

"Emma," I whispered. "I think we have to go out there."

"Just wait," she whispered back. "Don't you want to hear what they're going to say to each other?"

I could hear the leaves rustling, the distant traffic from the main road. Some unknown energy flowed through my veins, and my heart pounded with the pressure of it. Everything between them could go wrong in the blink of an eye. "No, not if they're going to fight."

"But what if—"

"No. I've got to go," I told her firmly. "Now. Come on."

We stepped out from behind the building and immediately saw Rex had stopped in the path. Seeing Rex stop, Will turned and stared.

"Look, I'm sorry," I said to Rex as we reached him. "The two of you are in danger, so watching you both meet furtively in a closed construction site in the middle of the night? Not something I can stand by and watch." I positioned myself between the two men as Rex eyed me strangely.

"Who are you?" Will stared as if he couldn't quite place me. Then his face fell. "You were at the police station. Both of you." He looked back and forth between Emma and me. "You're cops. Probably his cops."

Emma didn't answer.

Will reeked of sweat, his shirt soaked through, his breath heavy and labored and stinking of whiskey. "Will," I said with concern. "What are you doing? What do you think you're doing?"

Will's fear was palpable. He held the bottle of whiskey in his hand and pulled at his loafers, which had sunk into the muddy ground. He opened his mouth several times to speak, but his voice wouldn't come out.

"Just take a deep breath, try and calm yourself, and tell us," Emma added. "We're not here to hurt you, dude."

"I'm trying to find a way out of this mess I've got myself into," he told us as he lurched drunkenly in my direction.

Rex took a step forward as if to defend me, but I laid my hand on his chest as he went to step past. My other hand reached to push Will back gently. "Why don't you tell us about the mess, Will? Maybe the three of us can help you."

"No one can," he complained and took another swig. The light was dim, and Will's face was pale as he struggled to keep the bottle of whiskey balanced.

"What did you think you would find here?"

He looked bewildered, the result—no doubt—of the whiskey.

"His mind is awash in that liquid," Rex said, pointing toward the bottle in Will's hand. "He can barely string a sentence together, much less a cohesive thought or plan. I'm quite surprised he made it over here in one piece."

"We followed him in the Jeep to make sure he was okay. Well, and to see where he went," Emma told him, and then her face flashed anger. "Speaking of which, you freaking car thief—where is my Malibu? If you so much as got a scratch on my car, Rex, I swear I will kill you myself."

"Do we really need to do this now?" I asked her, exasperated.

"I didn't want to put the two of you in any danger. Besides, this is clearly all my fault," Rex said. He looked at Will as if the souse would lunge at any second. (Though, to be fair, vampires on alert looked at everyone like that.) "I was the one that brought Amadeus Bozeman here for this project. He would never have come if I hadn't."

"Yeah, I don't think that's the case, Rex." I

looked at Will. "You said you've known Amadeus Bozeman for years. How?"

"I'm not drunk," Will insisted. "And I'm not a bad driver."

I sighed, held out my hand, and made a star. "Sober up Will Fisher immediately," I told it. It did a little excited shimmy and launched itself toward Will Fisher's head.

Will swatted at it like a fly.

For all the good it did.

Rex gently grabbed the flailing man to help stabilize him, but that only made Will panic more. "Get off me! Get off me! What is it?" he shouted. Then, with a wild aim, he slammed his whiskey bottle into Rex, and it shattered.

I wrinkled my nose at the even more pungent smell. "Just relax. It will be over in a second," I told him.

Will tumbled to the ground, his head shimmering with the star's magic. He coughed and sputtered for a minute, maybe two. Then, finally, he was still, his eyes clear. "What the hell did you just do to me?" the former insurance agent shouted as he climbed to his feet. "Who are you people?"

"Now maybe we can get some answers," Emma said.

"I want my lawyer," he told her. His cheeks were sunken, his skin pale, his features worn. His eyes were tired, bloodshot, and the air around Will was filled with the sickly sweet smell of booze. "I shouldn't talk to you without him."

"I'm almost sure you really don't want your lawyer," I mumbled.

CHAPTER FIFTEEN

My steps sank into the soft, soggy ground as the four of us gathered behind the parked construction equipment to talk. "What did you do to me?" Will Fisher asked as he heaved himself up on the dirty yellow metal step. "What was that light? Are you a vampire?"

"No, I'm not a vampire," I said, frowning. "Witch," I pointed to myself. "Cop, vampire," I added, pointing to Emma and then Rex. "Suspect," I said, pointing back to Will. "We know about your problems with your brother. We know you claim to be framed for the stolen painting. We know the insurance agency is some kind of a money-laundering front." I didn't explain how we knew any of that.

"Well, I'm sure you do," Will responded with a startled glare. "And him, too, since he's a vampire and got his money from us." Will's eyes turned hard as he considered each of us. "In fact, if two out of three you people are paranormals, you shouldn't even be chasing me at all. You know exactly what Jerry's doing." He paused, waiting for us to say something, but none of us did. "Are you gonna make me say it? You people always tell me not to say anything, and now you want me to talk in front of a cop? What is this?"

"You're right, Mr. Fisher. We know exactly what Jerry's doing," Rex said, quickly stepping forward to take charge. "And we know exactly what you're doing. But now, we need to know how much you understand about what Jerry's doing. In fact, I'm surprised that Jerry hasn't asked you himself."

Emma shifted on her feet and looked slightly confused, but she remained silent as we watched the exchange between Rex and Will.

"Well, that vampire rarely comes out of his lair, anyway, right? If I hadn't seen him and Miranda at the beginning of all this?" He sighed and settled his back against the top step of the large metal machine. "Look, I'll tell you whatever you want. I just want to make sure that my wife isn't killed by the Vampire Collective. That's my only goal anymore."

The what now?

"I'm sorry, did you say the Vampire Collective?" I asked him.

"Please. It's not like you've never heard of it," Will scoffed.

It was exactly like I'd never heard of it.

Because I'd never heard of it.

"Why don't you explain to us what you know about the Vampire Collective, Mr. Fisher? As I've already said, we'd like to know what you know." Rex's lips lightly parted, and his fangs glinted like steel in the moonlight. "Please don't make me ask again," the vampire added coldly.

Will closed his eyes, seeming to consider his next words carefully. "Vampires aren't people like anyone else, right? They aren't even human."

Well, this was starting off fantastically educational.

"Vampires travel in packs, like wolves, and the Collective is just the biggest pack in the world. It's huge. All vampires belong to it. And once we humans know about them? If they don't eat us, we have to do what they say." Will's voice had shifted to a more disgusted tone. He looked up at Emma. "Oh. Right. Now I get it."

I'm glad he got it.

Because I didn't.

Vampires didn't travel in packs. It was like this guy had gotten his education from watching eighties vampire movies. And there was no organization I'd ever heard of called the Vampire Collective. If there had been, we would've known about it at the Ministry. No rules about humans being subservient to vampires. Nothing this guy said had any basis in any reality I had ever heard of.

"I'm still a little confused. So the vampires glamoured you?" Emma asked Will.

Will's eyes flicked around uncomfortably as if he was trying to figure out if Emma's question was serious or a trap. "I don't know what that even means. The Collective has an ancient secret society of human collaborators. There are very few of us, you know. It's supposed to be a real honor."

"Of course," I agreed with him to keep him talking. "How did you get to join?"

"I didn't know when I took this job that the insurance agency was part of it. When Jerry told me? He said we would get all kinds of money and things that most human beings never get to have. So I said yes. Brought my brother in, too." His face fell. "But once you're in, you take an oath, and then you can't leave. Ever." Will leaned in and whispered conspiratorially. "A few years ago, they actually made our owner a vampire."

"Jerry?" Rex asked.

Will nodded. "And look, Sullivan, I didn't want to leave because I wanted to break my oath to the vampires or anything. My wife found a rehab out in California." The man looked down at his feet. "I drink too much. I mean, I know I'm a drunk. I don't know how it happened, but it did."

"Those habits can sneak up on you and become addictions without you noticing," I told Will sympathetically.

"Yeah, well, I've been drinking too many years to quit on my own, and my Gloria? Gloria won't have a baby unless I get it under control." He looked up, his eyes shining with unshed tears. "I was just looking for my employment contract to see if there was anything in the oath I signed that would let me get out of here for two months. Just a short leave, you know? Because my brother wasn't gonna let me."

"And you found something when you were looking for your contract that you weren't supposed to have seen," I guessed.

Will looked at me with a strange mixture of

surprise and fear. "Yeah. That's exactly what happened. Jerry told me the Collective was furious. He knows what I found," Will said, pointing at Rex.

Because all vampires were members of the Collective, you know.

I couldn't believe these people got so snowed.

"It's why they framed me for stealing a painting that never even existed in the first place. If Charles wasn't my brother, I'd probably be dead already." The man looked at Rex with desperate eyes. "I told him that I would never betray the Vampire Collective, I'd never tell anybody what you've got on this property—"

"What do I have on this property?" Rex asked, his voice gentle.

Will's eyes darted over to Emma.

"You can speak freely in front of her," he told the nervous man.

"When I was looking for my employment contract in Miranda's desk, I found the plans for the underground storage and prison lair," he admitted. In the pale moonlight, Will Fisher looked defeated and frightened. "I wasn't snooping, I swear. I wouldn't have told anybody about it. I mean, I've known that what we do isn't strictly legal for years, and I never said a word. I would never cross the vampires." He shrugged unhappily. "But Charles didn't believe me."

"Hold on, back up. What's in the underground storage?" Emma asked.

"All the stuff vampires want to hide from other people," he told her as if it should be apparent. "Things that their 'other lives' owned that need to get transferred into this one. The money that has to be moved around. You know, that kind of stuff."

"So...they framed you for stealing a painting that didn't exist to ensure that if that underground storage area was found, the blame would rest solely on you," Emma surmised. "That insured you couldn't tell anyone, and they could pin the whole thing on you." She nodded as if she took Will's silence for a yes. "That's pretty smart."

Will looked crestfallen.

"Oh, buck up," the detective told him. "I didn't say they were going to get away with it. I just said it was smart."

"Excuse me, when you were describing what you found, did you say there was a prison lair?" Rex asked.

"Did I?" Will looked stricken. "Was I not supposed to mention that, sir?" the insurance agent asked in a panicked voice. "I'm so sorry, sir.

You told me that I could speak freely, and that's what I found, and I didn't mean to break any—"

"Stop," Rex said, and I felt the tingly energy of the vampire's glamour on the frightened man. "Sit here, and let us talk among ourselves for a moment. You're not to move. Remain calm, breathe deeply, and enjoy the quiet."

Will nodded vigorously. Then he took a deep, cleansing breath.

"OKAY, OUT WITH IT," Emma whispered to her brother. "What the heck is a Vampire Collective?"

Rex's eyes landed on me. "Do you have any idea what he's talking about?"

I shook my head. "I've never heard of this Vampire Collective. And honestly, all of the words he was using to describe vampires? They were wrong. Vampires don't travel in packs. They're not werewolves. Everything I know about vampires says they're pretty solitary. The only halfway organized group I knew about was the one you were associated with out in Las Vegas."

"And even we were relatively solitary," Rex admitted. "We were each assigned to a particular human in the organization or sent out on assignments alone." His pale face glanced back toward Will. "He believes that he's telling the truth, and I can scent no other vampire on him in the recent past. But, whatever the man believes? He's been convinced of it by circumstances and statements. Not vampire glamour."

"So what do we think is happening here, magical creatures from the great beyond?" Emma asked.

Rex and I both turned to stare at her.

"What? You are. I don't have any experience with this. You were in the paranormal government, and you were in the seedy paranormal underbelly of magical criminal organizations," Emma told both of us cheerfully. "Between the two of you, you have to be able to figure this out."

"It sounds to me like someone made up this big, organized vampire organization to scare these people into toeing the line," I told the two of them. "Nothing he said resembled any reality I'm aware of."

"Who made it up?" Emma asked.

Rex looked at me. "Amadeus Bozeman?"

I shook my head. "I wouldn't be surprised if he had something to do with this, but five years ago when Jerry Barber turned into a vampire? Bozeman still had his nose up the Witch Council's butt. Mina World, the witch he played lapdog to, hated vampires." There was no way an ambitious social climber like Amadeus Bozeman would have jeopardized his position with the most politically powerful witch in the paranormal world by cavorting with vampires. "However this started, it started before Bozeman got involved."

"How did you get involved in this?" Emma asked Rex. "Did you just apply for a loan at some vampire bank and got referred to the insurance agency?"

"More than that happened, though. The money is just one part of it. Bozeman told Rex I killed his friend," I said, thinking out loud. Turning to him, I held out my hand. "Bozeman wanted you here, he wanted you angry at me, and he wanted Emma and me busted up as a crime-fighting duo. And he wanted all that a month and a half ago."

"And he wanted me to build on this land," Rex reminded us.

All three of us turned toward the back of the property.

"It seems to me everything has been about

coming up with plausible alternate suspects for what's going on back there. And not just in the human world," Emma said as the three of us stared. "In the human world, the alternate suspect is Will Fisher." Emma turned and looked at her brother. "In the paranormal world, Rex, the alternate suspect is you."

Rex turned toward his sister with surprise.

"Think about it. If what they have locked up in that little tiny cinderblock box with the door makes the paranormal world angry? Well, you're the vampire that owns nearly all the land around it. You have a business relationship with the Barber Insurance Agency. It would be effortless to blame you for what's going on back there."

"I can see your point, but what's going on back there?" I asked.

"Theft is not going to raise an eyebrow in the paranormal world. Neither is money laundering." Rex asked. "It's just not. No one cares about financial crimes."

"He's right," I told Emma. "Most paranormals don't care about money."

"Most isn't all," Emma pointed out.

Rex thought for a moment. "Will Fisher doesn't know much more than what he said. The only thing I can tell you about that tiny box building is that it's much bigger on the inside. It really is just the entrance to an underground area, at least according to the plans Will found."

"With a bunch of cells," I reminded them both. "The paranormal world may not care about money laundering or theft, but you know what it does care about? Kidnapping and murder, especially of paranormals."

"Especially if that kidnapping and murder is done by a human to a paranormal," Rex added with a nod. "It goes to historical fear. The paranormal world is trying to reintegrate back into the world somewhat, with the loosening of the penalties for proof of our existence. But if you take a look at modern media? Not a peep about us."

I nodded. "No one's running out to do an interview with Oprah. It doesn't matter what restrictions have been loosened."

"We are still somewhat cautious," Rex told his sister.

"Got it," Emma said. "Thanks for the paranormal current political events *Reader's Digest* version. Again. Because I've heard this all from both of you before. I get it. Heard it, get it, and sorry your people are going through... whatever. But—and I say this with much love and respect for you both—I simply don't care." Emma pointed with her chin across the clearing. "None of what you just told me explains anything about what's going on in that box. I'm trying to solve a crime here, not write an anthropology paper."

Ouch.

"You technically solved the crime, though," I pointed out. "You're in charge of finding the stolen painting and prosecuting the person that stole it. There's no painting, so no case and no one to prosecute."

Emma stared at me with astonishment. "Why, because old Grog McDrunkard over there told me there was no painting, and he was framed? I don't know how it is in the paranormal world, Astra, but guilty people usually blame someone else for their crimes. Especially when I'm the one asking them about it."

WE WALKED BACK over to Will Fisher.

"How do we get in the little box?" Emma asked him.

His face turned white. "I can't tell you that. My brother, Charles, will kill my wife if I tell the police how to get in there! But, I told you, I'm not supposed to know about that place! The fact that I do is the whole reason I'm in all this trouble!"

Emma stood over the man, her features hardening. "Unless I know what's in that place, I have no way to prove whether you're telling the truth or not. So if you don't want to go to prison for stealing a painting Miranda Barber swears existed, I need to get in that underground lair."

"Jerry is there, and he's a vampire! He'll kill you!"

"I have my own vampire." Emma hitched her thumb toward Rex. "He won't let anybody kill me."

"Not for long, though," Rex murmured, glancing at the sky. "It is slightly past three a.m. If you want my assistance with whatever you're going to do, you're going to need to do it quickly. Sunrise starts a little after six-thirty, and I need to be underground by then."

"Convenient, then, that we have an underground vampire lair just a little bit that way," Emma told her brother. She turned back toward Will. "Surely Jerry would want to help another vampire out, wouldn't he? Since they are all members of this gigantic Vampire Collective thing?"

"Why is it always called a lair for vampires?" I

asked no one in particular. "I've always wondered that. Lair. It just sounds so ominous."

"Because it is defined as a place where a wild animal, especially a fierce or dangerous one, lives. In Scotland, it's also a burial plot in a graveyard," Rex explained with a shrug. "The word works on both levels."

"Witches live in a hearth," I told him.

"Likely because witches dislike the cold," the vampire offered.

"Or we like to burn things," I deadpanned.

"You two want to re-join the conversation over here?" Emma asked, exasperated.

"I thought you decided we're going over there," I said, pointing toward the small building. "I'm just waiting for you to stop talking about it and start walking."

The detective glared at me and began walking.

WE WERE HALFWAY to the river when Archie flew toward us.

"Where have you been?" I asked.

"It's an owl," Will said, confused. "Where else would it be?"

"I've been watching Jerry and his van and his

little tiny box," Archie said as he flew circles over us. "There's been nothing for hours. No movement, nobody coming and going. I was starting to feel like I made the wrong decision to go watch it. Because nothing."

I shrugged. "Well, at least we know there's been nothing going on down there."

"For hours. Though there's a lot of mice down by the river, did you know that?" The owl continued flying in lazy circles, his silent wing flap undermined by the loud smacking of his beak. "Just when I thought nothing would happen and all the mice had figured out they needed to run for the hills? He came out."

"Who came out?" Emma asked.

"Jerry," the owl answered. "He's walking this way."

"Is he alone?" Rex asked.

"Yep, just him and a bunch of mice cowering in fear from my mighty hunting skills. There may be a snake or two, but I don't like snakes. They're too wiggly." Archie sailed over and landed on Rex's head. He bent over and looked into Rex's eyes, his head upside down. "Why do you ask?"

"If he's alone, why is he walking?"

Emma stopped and turned. "I don't understand. What do you mean?"

Rex disappeared from underneath Archie in the blink of an eye—which the owl was not expecting. Feathers flew everywhere as Archie squawked and tumbled to the ground.

"Are you okay?" I asked, concerned.

"You know, I'm the goddess's own owl!" Archie shouted into the night angrily. "You should show me some more respect, fang-face!" He rolled off his back, his feathers flapping in agitation. "Don't know what the goddess was thinking, wanting you to survive," the owl muttered as he retook flight. "One less vampire in the world couldn't matter that much."

Suddenly, Rex reappeared. "I ran one mile away and one mile back in the few seconds I was gone," he explained. "No vampire would bother to waste time walking if they were alone and no one was there to see them disappear. There would be no reason to. He wouldn't have to slow down to allow for anyone that needed to keep up."

"Maybe he just felt like walking?" Emma asked.

"I am telling you. He's walking like a human for a reason," Rex insisted. "We have a natural pace, and human speed is not that pace."

"Or he's not actually a vampire at all," I added.

Eight eyes stared at me in shock.

"Look, we don't know for sure that he's a vampire. We just know he claims he is, and everybody thinks he is. And we know he's supposed to be dead, but people can fake something like that pretty easily." I held up my hands. "But we have no proof the dude is actually a vampire."

Archie nodded and bobbed his head. "That explains it."

"Explain what?" Rex asked.

"That would explain why he needs the gun he's carrying."

CHAPTER SIXTEEN

*T*he four of us—and Archie—walked a few minutes south of the construction site and hid among some large boulders and trees.

Well, Archie flew.

We walked.

The rocks clawed out from the rubble along more giant fissures of stone. It looked like they had caved in on themselves and now sat like fairy tables.

Once well hidden, I rummaged through my bag and tossed an attraction crystal out into the center of the clearing just beyond the ragged edge. It was about the size of a fist and flat, brown in color with multicolored shimmering swirls that faded as soon as it landed.

Once assured it was nearly invisible, I crossed my fingers that was enough of a plan. Because we honestly didn't have much of one.

"Are you sure that will work?" Emma asked.

"Any human with evil intent within three hundred feet will be pulled to that spot," I told her with a nod. "If Jerry's got a gun and he's human, he will literally walk right to it as long as he gets within range of its pull." I looked over at Will sitting contentedly on the ground, more comfortable now that a large rock shielded him from the view of his old boss. "Huh. Good to know, I guess."

"He has no evil intent?" Emma asked.

"Not at the moment, no."

"And if Jerry's a vampire? What then?"

I bit my lip and glanced toward Rex. "I have something I can use, but I'd prefer not to. If we have any other options. It's just…" I trailed off and tried to figure out how I would admit that I had a magical military device that Rex's entire species felt should be outlawed, put in a pile, and destroyed. "Well, anyway, if we don't, I can deal with it, but—"

"You have *vampire twine*." Rex's tone was gut-wrenched, and yet under that remained the enticing and dreadful desirability all vampires had. His eyes widened, and his pained frown deepened into an angry scowl. "Admit it. You're carrying vampire twine."

Emma looked confused. "Someone needs to clue me in. What's vampire twine?"

"Vampire twine is an enchanted military capture device," Rex spat before I could answer. "The Witches' Council wanted to ensure that when their thugs went out to capture a vampire, there was no chance for that vampire to escape. None." He glared at me. "The vampire twine renders a vampire utterly defenseless. Paralyzed, helpless, vulnerable—and yet completely conscious of the agency that's been stolen from them for added humiliation."

I wanted to defend it, argue with his characterization…but I couldn't.

Emma looked at me. "Is that true? Is that how it works?" She did her best to use her nonjudgmental detective voice, but I could see the concept horrified her. "And do you have some of that stuff?"

When I learned about it in the Academy, I was shocked that we had something like that in our arsenal and could use it with impunity against suspects or any vampire that got in our way. As I've mentioned before, the Witches' Council wasn't the most friendly group of ladies you could meet. Probably why they were overthrown.

I understood Rex's unhappiness. However, it didn't change the fact that it was the most effective defense against a vampire trying to kill someone.

I sighed.

"It is, and I do," I admitted.

Her face turned the color of fog. "Astra, you do realize in the human world, use of that stuff would probably be an international war crime. So why would you carry something like that?"

"It's just for emergencies. Like this one." I glanced at Rex, who was watching me carefully. "Stop looking at me like that. I've never used it. Not once. And yes, I get your aversion to it. It is nasty, nasty stuff. That's also what makes it so effective."

Rex crossed his arms.

"I'd also like to point out I've also never drug a human along on one of my missions." I glanced from Rex to his sister. "If a vampire comes at Emma and tries to bite her?" I said, pointing. "You can bet I'm going to be flinging some twine, dude. It doesn't do any permanent damage."

"Not physically. The psychic wounds for a vampire—"

"Are likely not as bad as the physical wounds of a vampire killing a human being, or turning them to a vampire when they don't want to become a vampire."

"Who would want to become a vampire?" Emma asked in a breezy tone. She looked at Rex and smirked with self-assurance. "I mean, besides you. Because I've always known you were weird."

"You'd be surprised," he told her. "There are humans that go in search of vampires to beg them for the immortal life." Rex's frowned. "Sometimes, the situation can get out of hand. Humans can be strange."

"He's about a quarter-mile away and coming right for you," Archie called from above. "Maybe he's a human after all! Or, you know, a vampire coming to kill you all. I mean, in either of those scenarios? He would come straight for you. So prepare for both."

"Wow, that was loud," Will said. "The screech sounded like a child screaming." He shuddered. "Creepy."

"Will, you need to be quiet now," I told him. "I'm just guessing Jerry's not a vampire. But, if he is a vampire, he'll be able to hear you when he shows up. So let's not give ourselves away."

"If he is a vampire, he'll be able to hear all of us right now from where he is," Rex pointed out. "There's no way we will be able to hide from him."

The entire group actually settled down, grew quiet, and listened to the night for indications Jerry was approaching the clearing.

The crickets chirped loudly, and the breeze blew the scent of flowers in full bloom as we waited. Then, finally, I looked up to find the horizon held just a subtle, tiny hint of color—a warning that the sun was on its way from the other side of the world and our clock was ticking.

THE SUPPOSED corpse known as Jerry Barber walked straight to the clearing's center and practically stepped on the attraction crystal with his right foot. "Why did I come here again?" he murmured to himself. He rubbed his eyes with his fists, grimaced with distaste, then jerked his head back as he whacked himself with a large black gun. "Ow. Frick. I can't remember why I came here. Oh, right. Where is he?" Jerry scanned the clearing. "He told me he'd be here."

"Human," I whispered.

"Yes. I'm not blind. He's meeting someone, and it's not us," Rex added.

"I'm not deaf," I whispered back.

"Would you two shut up? Just stay down. Let's see what he says," Emma scolded.

"To who?"

As if on cue, Amadeus Bozeman stepped into the clearing like a tourist at a garage sale who knows he'll be cool as soon as he can pick up what he wants and be somewhere else. "Friend, I'm afraid you've been had," the witch told Jerry.

"What are you talking about?" Jerry asked.

Bozeman marched with purpose to the center of the clearing, pushed Jerry lightly back, and grabbed the attraction crystal from the ground. His eyes shined with a hint of humor as he tossed it in the air once, then held it out to Jerry. "I told you it was important for us to get Astra out of the way. Her military-issued tools are quite powerful and designed to overcome magical defenses." Bozeman raised his voice and looked around. "Isn't that right, Astra?"

I stood up from behind the rock.

"Astra, what are you doing!" Emma hissed, her hand reaching up.

"Astra, stop!" Rex said, jumping up with his arms out. Then, with one quick movement, he shoved me behind him. "Leave her alone. She has no part of this. I was the one that agreed to borrow money from the Barbers. This is clearly my fault."

I wanted to turn Rex around and kick him in a delicate part of his anatomy, but I wasn't sure that action had any effect on vampires.

What he did was chivalrous, sure.

But dumb.

Rex Sullivan seemed to have forgotten that I was bulletproof, well trained in dealing with violent witches, and was actually the one that was supposed to be protecting him.

"You really are all instinct, aren't you?" I muttered.

Bozeman's glare snapped to Rex instantly, and his eyes narrowed. "Who else is back there, I wonder?" the witch mused.

"What do you care?" I taunted back.

Jerry shook as he eyed the vampire. Sweat dotted his forehead, and his eyes cast about wildly for any other threats surrounding the clearing. "You told me that this would go off without a hitch, you idiot," the human glowered, his expression caught between fury and fear. "You said the other vampires wouldn't know. I swear, my wife told me to never trust a lawyer, and she was right. You're an idiot. That's a vampire, stupid, and I don't have any more vampire twine!"

Huh.

Vampire twine.

Why would these two need vampire twine?

That brought me up short.

"Gerald, do shut up, would you?" Bozeman asked politely—but menacingly.

"I know we're all under a lot of stress right now, but I have a really quick question." I stepped out from behind Rex. "How does a supposedly dead human being know about vampire twine? Most of your asset management and money laundering was for vampires, wasn't it, Barber?"

He looked at me with an expression I could only describe as panic. "How do you know that?" I stared and waited. "What's your point?" Jerry asked.

"Well, they wouldn't tell you about it. Vampires want all of that stuff shoved in a pile and burned, never to be seen again. That's how much they hate it. Hades, it's possible they would kill you just for having it," I mused out loud.

"More than possible," Rex told the men furiously.

"They wouldn't kill me! And when I turn into a vampire, they'll understand why I had to do what I had to do!" he shouted angrily. With the attraction crystal now in Bozeman's hands, Jerry kept pace with Amadeus's slow steps toward our hiding spot. Barber's gun flashed in the moonlight. "They won't get mad at me when I'm one of them! How can they?"

"Is that your goal?" I asked, slowly moving myself to step in front of Rex. "This past five years, it's all been about setting yourself up to turn into a vampire?"

"No," Jerry answered with a snort. "I had to fake my death because an idiot brownie got careless with the money we washed for them, and the cops were getting too close. Once I went underground, though, I thought to myself—Jerry, I said, why not get someone to turn you? You deserve it. Why just get money for dealing with all of this paranormal stuff? Why not get immortality, too?"

"It's five years later," I pointed out. "You're not a vampire. What happened?"

Jerry waved his arms in furious circles as the two continued stepping closer and closer. "Those stupid bloodsuckers wouldn't turn me! All those years, all those risks we took to help them, and when I needed something, did they help me?" he asked, his wild eyes bloodshot and angry. "Of course not. All those people we fixed up. All that money. They refused me. Me!" he shouted with indignation, thumping his chest. "They all refused me. Until Mozart over here."

I glanced at Amadeus Bozeman.

Mozart, huh?

"Mozart" looked utterly serene. Actually, it was more than that. He looked pleased with himself as Jerry outlined his complicity.

"What did you do, Bozeman?" I asked.

"I did assist Mr. Barber with the plan. It was fairly complicated, of course, but I'm used to political intrigue." Everything about Mozart Bozeman was as cool as a dream about polar bears. There wasn't so much as a bead of sweat on his brow. "Things seemed to be going off without a hitch. Well, until Will Fisher went poking around. You got closer to the truth than I expected you would, Astra. You were quite a fly in the ointment of my...our riches."

Emma continued to crouch down, her gun out

of her holster and gripped tightly in her hand. Will Fisher curled up in a ball, his face buried in his hands, next to her. His hands were slapped over his own mouth.

"Oh, yeah?" I asked. "How so?"

"I'd heard about your little goddess skill from others," Bozeman said as he stopped on the other side of the rock. "I knew you could possibly interfere, that some god somewhere could decide we didn't deserve what we both know we do." He glared at Rex to my right. "Rex was less helpful in that regard than I'd expected."

"Bite me," Rex spat at him.

The witch's laugh rumbled like a well-oiled engine. "Cute. Quite ironic, that insult. In any case, once I realized Jerry's greatest desire in the entire world was to become a vampire, we came up with a scheme to force a vampire to change him. I'd hoped the drama with Rex and his little human sister would keep you three occupied, at one another's throats, and out of our way." He frowned. "Since none of you are dead, clearly that was a miscalculation."

The boulder was torso high and about ten yards wide. Rex and I were visible chest up, but I suspected Jerry and Amadeus could not see

Emma or Will Fisher. It was hard to be sure, though.

"What do you mean, force someone to change him?" Rex asked.

"Oh, just provide a little bit of incentive. You know, put my thumb on the scales just a tad," Bozeman said with a cold smile as he leaned against the rock.

"What kind of incentive?" Rex asked.

"You can't read it from his mind, can you?" Amadeus Bozeman asked Rex with a conspiratorial whisper. "Try as you might, that information is a bit closed off from you, isn't it?" Then, turning to me, he winked. "The weapons cabinets were handy back at the Ministry, weren't they?" Then he frowned again. "Had that idiot Fisher not found the plans in Miranda's desk, this would have gone off without a hitch."

"You people really were a menace, you know that?" Rex spat at both of us.

I held out my hand, quickly made a fist, and opened it up. The star twinkled and floated, waiting for its assignment. "I want every magical block, forced blank, and protection taken off of Jerry Barber's mind so Rex can rummage through," I said quickly.

"What magic was that?" Bozeman raised his

eyebrow. He looked curious but not particularly concerned. "Quite shiny, though obviously more ambitious than you're capable of."

As if sensing that time was of the essence, the star flew out of my hand and blasted up Barber's nose. Within two seconds, Rex roared like a beast unleashed and lunged for the armed man. I tried to hold him back, but it was like a fly trying to stop a raging buffalo.

"Where is she?" Rex demanded. "How do I let her out?"

"Now, now, Mr. Sullivan," Bozeman said with slick concern. "It's a biometric lock, and if he's dead, you'll never see her again." Rex froze. The witch turned toward me, his expression black. "That was unexpected. You seem to have learned a new trick, my dear. I am glad I have contingencies."

"Rex, what's going on?" I asked, pulling him away from Jerry and back across the boulder. I was grateful he allowed me to because if he hadn't, I never could have moved him.

"He wants money," Rex growled. "Bozeman, I mean. He came to Forkbridge to help Barber get what he wanted. A vampire under his control. A vampire he could threaten. In payment, he would get all this vampire's money." Rex shook off my hands and pointed toward the two in a threatening manner. "The Barbers knew how to steal. They knew how to steal the money. Jerry couldn't steal the immortality, but they could wrap a vampire in vampire twine and refuse to let them out until they turned him."

"Val!" I burst out. "You idiots captured a vampire and wrapped them in vampire twine? For a month and a half?" I asked incredulously. "Are you out of your mind?"

"What's a month and a half in an immortal life, really?" Bozeman shrugged.

"Where is she?"

Bozeman yawned.

Rex turned and glanced toward the river. "She's locked in that box in the underground along with the spoils of their theft."

"Yeah, and only I can get in!" Jerry announced proudly.

I held out my hand, closed it, and opened it to another eager star. "Put the two of them to sleep until I wake them up again."

"The hell you will! Stupid magic people!" Jerry lifted his gun and pointed it at Rex. I jumped in front of him and wrapped my arms around him. The bullets left the chamber as the star reached his forehead, and I felt a series of hard thumps between my shoulder blades.

Ow.

The bullets kept flying as Jerry collapsed, but the gunfire stopped once he reached the hard ground.

When the clearing finally fell silent?

Emma and I were bruised…

…but Will and Rex were both alive.

"This bullet has vampire twine in it," I told Rex as I held it up. "This would have torn you to pieces. I think. To be honest, I don't know what it would've done to you, but I can't believe it was anything good."

"Look, Astra, I appreciate you jumping in front of me and all, but we're wasting time." Rex had grabbed Jerry and slung him over his shoulder. "I'm going to go. Will the two of you be all right?"

"Go."

Before I finished the one-syllable word, Rex was gone.

"This was all about a witch that wanted to be wealthy and a human that wanted to be a vampire," Archie said as he flew up and settled on the rock. "People trying to get what they don't deserve. Yeah, I can see why Athena wanted everybody involved slapped senseless. She hates stuff like that."

Emma tilted her head. "Why is he hooting now?"

Archie and I turned to look at Emma. "You can't understand me?" the owl asked with surprise.

"He just talked to you. Could you understand?" I asked her.

She shook her head no. "Just a couple of hoots."

I frowned. "I wouldn't think the magic just...I don't know, expires like that." I looked at Bozeman snoring on the ground. "Do we need to be worried?"

"Remember what I told you?"

"I remember a lot of things you tell me," I responded.

"So, then, you know." The owl bobbed his head with certainty and looked like he considered the matter settled.

I waited.

He stared.

I stared.

He began preening his feathers vigorously.

"Archie, I have no idea what you're talking about."

"You never listen to me, do you? No, you don't listen," Archie said as he walked toward me. "You can only use that magic to assist you on a Star card case." The owl waved his wing. "She can't hear me because the case is over. Or, to be more precise, the threat is over. No one's life is in danger anymore. We did it. Want to eat a mouse in celebration?" His large eyes blinked. "I can grab you one."

I related what Archie said to Emma, and her face fell.

"Well, that's kind of a bummer. I was just getting used to him. It was kind of fun to be able to talk to an owl."

I looked at the sleeping Amadeus Bozeman and wondered what I was supposed to do with him. Emma couldn't exactly arrest him—and even if she did, he was such a slippery character I had no doubt his plotting and magic would spring him free quickly. Amadeus told me there was no court system in Paranormopolis anymore, but...I mean, it's not like his word could be trusted.

"Are you going to arrest his wife?" I asked Emma.

"Who, Will's?" Emma pointed to the crouching, shaking alcoholic.

"Not Gloria!" Will shouted.

"I'm not talking about your wife, dude." I sat next to him, smacked him on the arm, and ordered him to calm down. "I'm talking about Miranda Barber. We went through those papers, and she took several hundred thousand dollars for Jerry's faked death."

Emma thought for a minute. "Rex can wipe their memory of all this paranormal stuff, right? I mean, obviously. He twisted my head into a pretzel."

I nodded.

"Then yeah, I think both the Barbers are going to wind up in jail along with your brother, Charles," Emma told Will. "His name was on an awful lot of those papers, and I bet the Barbers will sell him out in a heartbeat to get a better deal." She leaned back against the rock and stretched. "I'll write it all up and let the prosecutor sort it out."

Suddenly, Rex appeared overhead. He leaned over the boulder, his face twisted with tension.

"Astra, we need your help," he said quickly, reaching down to yank me up off the ground. "Every time I try and take the vampire twine off of Val and the others, I...I, um..." Rex looked embarrassed. "Well, I pass out. Sort of. I freeze and fall down."

"The others?" I asked in shock. "What others?"

He nodded. "They have four vampires in that place." His eyes reddened as if he were about to cry—and crying wasn't really a capability vampires had. "They are all wrapped in vampire twine. I can't get it off. Please." His please had a note of desperation, and for a brief second, I wanted to give him a hug.

I looked down at Emma, and she nodded.

"Go, we'll be fine here."

CHAPTER SEVENTEEN

I returned Will Fisher to his house and wished him good luck in his attempt to explain to his wife, Gloria, the ins and outs of what happened—especially with the gaps in his memory and knowledge that Rex had shoehorned in there. As I pulled the Jeep into the road, I glanced in my rearview mirror to see a nightgowned Gloria with her arms wrapped around Will.

Maybe, just maybe, they would make it. Perhaps love would be enough to overcome their problems.

Well, that and, you know, a better lawyer.

I returned to the construction site just before sunrise and drove back toward the tiny cinder block building that was bigger on the inside. With five vampires, two suspects, and a rising sun, there just wasn't enough time to deal with anything that happened. So Emma and I helped the vamps hunker down for the day and decided we'd deal with everything after we all got some rest.

"She's stunning," the detective whispered, glancing at her brother and Val, wrapped in each other's arms. Blankets piled up around them, forming a nest in one corner of the industrial-looking common room. "He cares about her a lot, I think."

"You don't have to whisper," I told Emma. "They won't wake up even if you shout at them." Rex had convinced the other vampires we wouldn't hurt them, and on his word, they all trusted us to be here with them. I was a little in awe, actually.

I'd never been in a vampire nest before.

Most non-vampires that had been didn't live long enough to tell the tale to anyone interested in hearing it.

"Right. I forgot, they can't hear me," she answered. "It's so weird. They don't breathe."

"Nope."

I looked at Rex and Val and audibly sighed with relief.

No one had been hurt; we all were alive—even the perps. While that was important, I was also grateful we'd made it through another assignment, and I didn't have to take anyone's life.

Such a strange, strange journey the past few days had been.

"You still mad at him?" I asked Emma.

"For what?"

"The whole mind pretzel thing," I reminded her.

"Oh." The detective looked surprised as her tired mind reached back to a few days ago as if the fight between them was a problem already long forgotten. "He and I are going to have a talk about it. That's for sure. A long one." Emma nodded at her brother, turned, and sat down on a cheap vinyl couch across from the two. "But I think a lot was going through his mind, though, you know? He thought you killed her; you were close to me. So I kinda get his reaction. Of course, he went about it the wrong way, but I think Rex meant well."

I nodded and yawned. "What should we do now? Call the captain?"

Emma looked at her phone. "If I call him now, they'll all show up here now, and we can't let them in with these vampires defenseless," she said, grabbing a pillow from behind her. "Let them sleep. We can get some sleep. You and I can get up this afternoon and look through this place, see if there's any evidence."

"Sounds good," I told her. I moved toward a vinyl recliner. "I locked the door already."

"Good. We'll deal with the rest of this mess when everyone wakes up, I think. The captain will just assume we're chasing after some lead." She laid her head down on an industrial-looking grey pillow and closed her eyes. A second later, they popped open again. "Hey. You need to call your family and let them know everyone's okay?"

"Archie went back to his roost in my room," I said. "He'll let them know."

"Good. I'm just glad that…all of this is over," she said, and then laid her head back, closed her eyes, and was breathing rhythmically in less than sixty seconds.

I pulled a medical blanket on top of me, took a deep breath, then exhaled slowly. My whole body felt like it had fallen into a pit of warm goo, the oddness of being relaxed for a change. The energy, the constant rush of anticipation, adrenaline, and fear had drained out of me. I felt like I could sleep for two days straight.

WHEN I OPENED MY EYES, a canopy of concrete and steel and shadows stretched above me.

"What?" I murmured, confused.

I sat up in my recliner, blinking in the dark and uncertain of where I was. The only light flooded in from the hallway outside the sizable utilitarian room. It cast the area in an eerie opposition of darkness and light. A heavy plastic smell lingered in the air, and every now and then, I caught a whiff of a...copper scent? Like old pennies.

Oh, right.

The vampire prison/stolen stuff storage facility underneath the little cinder block box. I wrapped myself tighter in the blanket and looked around. I had no idea how long I slept, but I felt groggy.

Emma lay on the couch next to my chair, still sleeping soundly. Jerry slumped over on the floor, his arms on his knees, facing the corner. Amadeus leaned against him, breathing with tense, shallow breaths. The only other sound (besides the steady breathing of those inhabitants that still required oxygen to survive) was the gentle hum of a machine in an adjacent room. I had no idea what it was.

The air felt dry and cold.

"Jeez, it really does look like a prison," I murmured.

"That was what it was intended to be," a woman's voice called from the other room. My head jerked up, and my heart seemed to clench in my chest at the sound of a voice I didn't recognize. "But now, thanks to you and your team, it will be a safe house for vampires traveling through Forkbridge. The first one, in fact, that has ever been here. You should be proud of yourself. Val and Rex will make this place from a curse into a blessing."

"Who's there?" I demanded, scrambling out of the recliner to stand up and look around. Emma's chest rose and fell as she breathed. Jerry and Amadeus were also quiet. Even Val and Rex and the other vampires, who were still sleeping, were silent and undisturbed by my shout and the woman's invasion.

"Come and see," she insisted.

"I'm not an idiot. If you want me to come to find you? That's precisely what I'm not going to do. Tell me who you are!" I demanded. I scanned the group again, glancing over at Emma, then Jerry, and Amadeus. None moved. None seemed awake. "Emma?" I hissed.

Nothing.

I marveled at her ability to sleep through a threat like this. I guess her honed instincts required at least eight hours of sleep to function.

"Fine," the invader responded with a resigned sigh. "Here I am."

She swept into the room from the area across the entrance door as if she'd been here all along. The woman's form was lit by a blue-white light coming from...somewhere. I scanned her intently, but I couldn't seem to make out a darned thing.

I couldn't place her age—she could have been anyone from a decade younger than me to a decade older, but she seemed...ageless. Something about her face, her eyes, her skin, the way she moved, it all added up to something... otherworldly. It was like I was getting a sense of her rather than seeing her.

"Who are you?" I asked. "What are you doing here?"

The woman laughed and circled the room, stepping lightly over the linoleum flooring as if her feet didn't need to touch the ground. She glanced at me occasionally, but her dark eyes never settled on me for more than a second. "They are all safe," she commented as she examined each sleeping form.

"Are you here to threaten that safety?" I asked, my body tensing. "Get out of here."

"Ah, no. No. No, no, no," the woman told me, her musical laughter threaded through her words. "I'm just here to admire your handiwork. You've done a wonderful thing." She stopped in front of where I stood. "You've proven that the living and the dead do not need to be enemies. Well done, Astra."

What on earth was this woman talking about?

I proved nothing. I just stopped a few bullets. I hardly thought what happened here would have a long-term effect on vampire-witch relations. Or vampire-human relations. Or any relations other than the ones between Emma, me, and the police department as we tried to explain this craziness.

She stepped toward me, and I instinctively put my hand up. "I don't know what you're talking about, lady, but you need to identify yourself."

"You're the most stubborn child, aren't you?"

I bristled at that. "You sound like my mother."

"I am as you perceive me," the woman said,

smiling mischievously. Then she winked. "A voice inside your head, a ghost in your imagination. Perhaps, if you listen to the things around you more, you might hear me more often."

Oh, great.

An apparition with a philosophy degree.

"Why are you here?" I asked again. I wasn't sure what game she was playing, so I didn't move.

"I am here to congratulate you," she told me, then looked up, and nodded. "I am here to congratulate you all, actually."

I looked at everyone else. "But they're asleep."

"As are you, my dear. Time to wake up!" She turned and glided toward the other side of the room, passing through a corner wall with no apparent effort.

I frowned. A ghost, maybe?

As soon as the question skittered across my mind, a flash of light enveloped me but...a light with mass. Strength. Substance and density. Awareness and agency.

It grabbed me from behind, hoisted me up off the ground, and then spun me around like a top. I struggled to break free. To kick, stomp, scream, anything.

But I couldn't escape.

I WAS STILL TOSSING and turning when the detective shook me awake.

"Are you okay?" she asked. "It looked like you had a bad dream."

I sat up, disoriented, and looked toward the corner of the room the mysterious woman disappeared through. Had it just been a dream? I touched my arm where the light had grabbed me. I could still feel the pressure of the grip, though it was fading.

Wow.

I must have really needed to sleep.

"Yeah, no, I'm good." Emma handed me some water. I sipped it and nodded. "I'm okay, really. Just a weird dream."

"Oh man, me, too," Emma admitted as she plopped down on the arm of my recliner. "This weird woman poofed out of thin air and started telling me all this weird stuff. It was crazy. Scared the heck out of me if you want to know the truth."

I froze. "What did she look like?"

Emma's face twisted as though the act of remembering those details was an effort equal to climbing up Mount Fuji with a blindfold on. "You know, I can't remember, really. I just remember her voice, and that she glowed—"

"—blue," I finished for her.

Emma blinked and jolted straight like she'd been zapped with a stun gun. "Yeah. An otherworldly blue. Kinda heavenly, almost." She tilted her head. "But how did you know that?"

I took another sip of water, then said, "I had the same dream. Well, to be more exact, I had the same woman visit my dream. I think. What did she tell you?"

"What to do with them," Emma said and pointed. "And that I should trust the captain with what went on here. Like, what really went on here. You?"

"She congratulated me and told me Val and Rex are going to turn this place into some kind of vampire sanctuary. Oh, and that the living and the dead can coexist. Or something."

Emma looked at me, then at everyone else. "I'd say that's weird, but working with you? Weird is starting to become par for the course. You're the wedge. Do you think it's anything we need to be concerned about?"

"At the moment?" I shrugged. "No. She told me that she came to see everybody, so I'll be really curious to find out what everyone else says when they wake up. We can deal with it then if there is anything to deal with."

She looked at her watch and nodded. "Okay. We have a few hours before they'll wake up. Let's see what's in the rest of this place."

AN ENORMOUS SIGN stood at the entrance of what could only be described as a dungeon, warning all those who entered not to feed the vampires. Emma and I had trouble speaking for a minute or two.

The large, horseshoe-shaped room had wooden planks every five feet or so. Dangling from the planks were huge, knotted globs of strings I knew must be vampire twine. It also hung from the ceiling, was wrapped around the doors…

Had any vampire managed to free themselves from their plank?

They wouldn't have been able to get far before being knocked out again.

Emma looked at me, her expression grim. "It's a holding area. This place is filled with stuff they used to catch and contain vampires." Though she was stating the obvious, it was like she needed to say it to believe it.

"I know. And it makes me wonder how large they were planning to make this operation if they needed a big sign at the door."

"I may not be paranormal, but I know what terrorist kidnapping stuff looks like. And this is it. Just despicable." She pointed to a door in the back of the room. "Let's check that out. It would make sense to hide the loot behind the vampires."

I nodded. "Yeah."

We opened the door to find a darkened warehouse-like room. Art was everywhere. Paintings, sculptures, glasswork, photography. There was just so much of it. Everything was in pristine condition—if a little dusty.

"This all must belong to the vampires," Emma said.

"That would be my guess."

She leaned against the wall and stared at it. The detective seemed overwhelmed. "How many years did it take for them to acquire this many things? And how am I supposed to explain all this to a small-town police department? This is all high-end fine art. This place is going to be crawling with feds. I just know it." Emma turned her face pale. "And how did they even build this without us noticing?"

"Well, think about it. Who's going to think something like this would be in Forkbridge?" I asked. Then I shrugged. "Like you said, it isn't the kind of place anyone comes to and stays. No one pays us much attention. We're a stop on the way from one place to another. If people even bother to stop."

I think we stood there for ten minutes just staring at all the stuff. Historical stuff. Stuff worth millions. Stuff that disappeared before the first world war. And the second. Property believed stolen by the Nazis. Just so much stuff. Sparkly, shiny, valuable stuff.

"The history in this room…"

"Yeah. I know," I agreed.

"And the government is probably going to confiscate it all because of the vampires…I mean, they are not alive. They can't fill out paperwork, right? I mean, can they? They can't be questioned during the day. So that's going to look suspicious, right?" Emma slammed back against the wall and crossed her arms. "What an absolute mess this is."

I could see Emma was getting overwhelmed.

"Hey, just relax. We'll figure this out. We always do."

For a long while, Emma didn't respond. Eventually, the detective cleared her throat, grabbed my hand, and pulled me away. "Come on," she said. "Let's check out the other rooms."

By the time we cleared the building, I had a good understanding of what had happened. Though, to be fair, I understood what happened before I ever set foot in this place. The scale of what Bozeman and Barber had planned?

It was ambitious.

I had to give them that.

CHAPTER EIGHTEEN

*E*mma told the captain pretty much all of it.

Harmon eyed Emma sternly with arms folded as she explained the ins and outs of the conspiracy. To my surprise the color remained in his face the entire time he listened, and his face stayed impassive. The leader of the Forkbridge Police Department was either one of the steadiest men I'd ever met, or one of the most practiced at looking like he was.

"And that's the story," Emma finished with a nod. "The dream told me I should tell you, and I have absolutely no idea why. But when everyone else here woke up with messages from the same person, I decided to go all in and take a chance.

Besides, it was way easier to do that than try and come up with a story to cover for all of this, anyway."

With calm eyes he scanned over each of my companions. "I see."

"Awesome." Emma smiled. "So, what do you think?"

The longer we waited for his observation and reaction, the more pronounced became the mental note in my head not to accept any poker night invitations from Captain Harmon.

"Well," Harmon said flatly, "that's quite a story."

"It is," Emma agreed, nodding. "If I were going to make something up, trust me, I'd have come up with something more believable. I know this sounds crazy, but those five over there? They are vampires. They kind of prove the story."

Rex leaned toward the captain and declared once again that I was innocent of any accusations he had previously shared. "I hope you can understand why I took the actions that I did," he nodded looking remorseful. "My sister and Astra are quite a formidable pair, and the visit I got told me unequivocally that I need to ensure they continue to work together."

"And that I should be paid," I added, even

though I had no idea if that was the case. Harmon glanced at me, his face still impassive.

"If we are not needed anymore," one of the vampires said, stepping forward and pointing toward the two vampires flanking him, "the three of us would like to leave here and let the rest of our family know that we are all right. We have been gone a long time." His expression was placid but his eyes were intense as he scanned everyone with a quiet challenge. Turning toward Rex, he held out his hand. "Thank you again for assisting in our rescue, brother. We owe you."

"What was your name again?" Captain Harmon asked.

"You don't need our names," the vampire responded sharply. "We know yours. If we need anything from you, Captain Harmon, we will find you." The nameless vampire pointed toward Rex. "He can answer any questions about us. He's well aware of what we are comfortable with and what is off limits. Val," he added, turning toward the woman standing next to Rex. "I'd obviously prefer—"

"You don't even need to say it," she told him fondly.

"Well, I am sorry that you were taken prisoner in my town, and we will do our best to make sure it doesn't happen again," Harmon answered, his brow furrowing. The captain seemed slightly unhappy with the idea of being left out of the loop and having information walk out the door, but on the other hand?

The three men were vampires, after all. Harmon probably didn't want any more involvement with them than he had to have.

Once the three were gone, he looked down at Amadeus and Jerry. "Do these two need paramedics?"

"No. Astra can wake them up as soon as we're ready."

"Emma, I know you've had a rough time of it, but how are you feeling now?" Harmon stepped forward to lay a hand on her shoulder. He gazed down at her with an almost fatherly concern. "You did just tell me your brother affected your own mind. I have some trepidations about trusting your story from beginning to end." He frowned. "Not the least of which is because I have no idea what I'm supposed to do if it is true."

"I can confirm Astra's family managed to free any hold that I had on Emma," Rex told him. The captain gave him a quick nod. "No vampires committed any crimes in your city, Captain Harmon. I know imprisoning us would be—"

"It would be crazy," Harmon barked at him. "I don't have the budget to keep vampires in jail, and you'd all go up like a Roman candle as soon as the sun rose. We try and make sure all the prisoners get yard time. We're not set up for this. Three hours ago I didn't even know this was possible."

"Captain, I have to say, you're taking this awfully well." Emma sounded more disbelieving than worried. "I've had nightmares trying to imagine how this would go down if I had to bring you into it."

Harmon looked mostly composed, but his expression changed just a bit as if a thought troubled him. In seconds, the concern disappeared again, hidden.

"I know I don't talk about my personal life much," Harmon answered, "but my life has gotten pretty strange lately." He moved back to the case before Emma could ask him for any more details. "I don't have any problem believing what you told me. Let's just leave it at that for now. You, Rex—you can wipe away any knowledge of the paranormal from these two, correct?"

Rex looked surprised, but gave Harmon a nod. "That one, though, is a witch. Paranormal powers can work oddly on the other paranormals. I can do it initially, but it likely wouldn't be permanent."

The captain made a thoughtful face. "I can deal with an honest-to-goodness witch but it's probably better that paranormals deal with paranormals," he decided. "If you can get the witches on board, I'll be more than happy to leave this one"—he pointed to Amadeus—"all to you guys."

"The witches?" I asked, my eyebrow raised.

"Well, it sounded much more professional than telling you to go ask your mom." He turned back to Rex. "Would you mind?" he asked, gesturing toward Jerry while pulling handcuffs from his belt. "I'd like to get someone in jail before the late show comes on."

"He wants us to deal with Amadeus?" Aunt Gwennie gestured toward the unconscious Bozeman face-down on the floor, his bum stuck up in the air. "Minnie, what could that man possibly expect us to do with him? Turn him into a mouse and feed him to Archie?"

"I vote for that one!" Archie said flying excitedly across the living room and landing with both talons on Amadeus's gluteus maximus. "Though if we are going to turn him into something tasty? Might I suggest—"

"You may not," my mother said sternly, cutting off. "You're not eating the witch, Archimedes."

"You people really are stick-in-the-muds sometimes, you know that?" Archie grumbled at my mother with disgust.

My mother and Aunt Gwennie stared at the sleeping man Emma and I had dumped on the floor. Mother wore a grumpy expression and Aunt Gwennie wore a horrified and slightly frightened one.

"I am quite gratified that the captain decided witches should deal with witches," my mother said finally. She nodded to herself. "It is proper, after all." She waved her hand in the air. "Besides, there's no human cell in the world that can hold this man." Her eyes narrowed. "He's a snake."

"Well, no," Archie pointed out. "If he was, I could eat him."

"The punishments of the others involved," Aunt Gwennie murmured. "What are the humans doing with them? You said that the Barbers were being arrested?"

Emma nodded. "And Charles Fisher. The three of them turned on each other once we got them down to the station, and all three will be going to prison for a long time. The state will probably take their money—unfortunately, the vampires won't get it back. As far as the state is concerned, it just looks like some organized crime money-laundering operation, and the government seizes that."

"What about all those things that you all found in the underground?" Ami asked as she walked toward us. "Can you get those back to the vampires they belong to?"

"Technically, they belong to Val," I pointed out. "They kidnapped and captured her to try and get her assets. That can take a while. Any companies she formed to hold them? They had to add the Barbers into those companies and then a few months later remove her so it didn't look suspicious."

Ami nodded. "I thought they told Rex she died?"

"They did," Emma told Ami. "But on paper, but she hadn't really entirely done so yet. That's probably why they kept her captive. Bozeman was so greedy, he kind of got ahead of himself. They just told Rex that to rile him up. They were still taking all her land, or companies, her money.

Turns out she actually owns the place she was being imprisoned in. Crazy, right?"

"Since she owns the place, they can start changing it into a decent place to live, and a place for other vampires to visit," I added. "We're going to go back later on tonight to remove the vampire twine for them."

"Vampire twine?" Ayla asked as she and Althea joined us. "Mom taught me about that a couple of years ago. That stuff is horrible! They tied them up with vampire twine?" Her apple-cheeked face twisted in dismay. "Where would human insurance agents get vampire twine?"

All seven of us looked down at the same time.

"We need to call Paranormopolis," Aunt Gwennie said automatically. "Firstly, so they can secure their dangerous paranormal weapons closet, because clearly they're not doing a good job right now. Second, they have a war crimes act targeted against anyone from the Witches' Council regime."

My mother nodded. "There is our answer. That stolen vampire twine's going to put Amadeus Bozeman in paranormal prison for the rest of his life." My mother lifted her slippered foot and pushed against the witch's sleeping form. "I can't think of anyone who deserves it more."

"I do. I deserve it more. He deserves to be a mouse. Or a duck. Or small fox. And I deserve to eat him." Archie stared up at my mother, wings in the realm of his hip area. "I am the goddess's own owl. I worked on this thing as much as everyone else did. I should get a reward."

"Yes, Archie, you did. But no one else that worked on this case is getting a reward, so why should you?" My mother pointed out, her face taking on an unusually sunny expression. "Surely you want what you did to remain in the realm of service to your goddess. After all, that is your purpose, is it not? Astra didn't even get paid this time."

"Though I did get my job back," I announced proudly. Everyone else smiled and congratulated me. "The captain felt that it might be a good idea to have a witch on the force considering the attention our little town has been getting from the paranormal world."

"How did the Barbers ever wind up dealing with vampires and paranormals, anyway?" Althea asked. "I don't think I've ever seen a vampire in Forkbridge, ever. I mean, they really stayed under the radar, right?"

"Since their memories have been wiped of all the paranormal knowledge they had, I'm not sure that we'll ever know," Emma pointed out.

WE WOULD COME to regret that decision. The choice to wipe information first and ask questions later.

But that's a story for another time.

THANK YOU FOR READING!

I hope you enjoyed Magic's a Hoot. Please think about leaving a review. Astra, Archie and the whole Arden family continue their adventures in Book 4, Heavy Meddle Magic.

KEEP UP WITH LEANNE LEEDS

Thanks so much for reading! I hope you liked it! Want to keep up with me?

Visit leanneleeds.com to:

Find all my books…

Sign up for my newsletter…

Like me on Facebook…

Follow me on Twitter…

Follow me on Instagram…

Thanks again for reading!

Leanne Leeds

FIND A TYPO? LET US KNOW!

Typos happen. It's sad, but true.

Though we go over the manuscript multiple times, have editors, have beta readers, and advance readers it's inevitable that determined typos and mistakes sometimes find their way into a published book.

Did you find one? If you did, think about reporting it on leanneleeds.com so we can get it corrected.

ARTIFICIAL INTELLIGENCE STATEMENT

Portions of this book were created with the assistance of AI tools used for editing, proofreading, and refining the text. However, the ideas, storyline, characters, and overall creative vision remain my own original work.

While some aspects of the cover image were generated using AI tools, it was done so under my creative direction and curation.

I want to acknowledge the use of these technologies as part of my creative process, while affirming that the essence of this work comes from my own imagination and effort.

Leanne Leeds